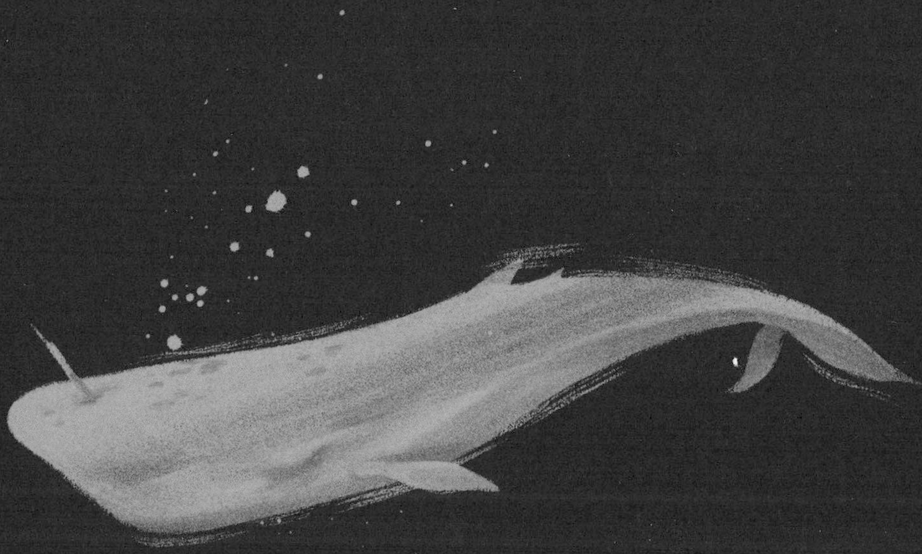

And The Ocean
Was Our Sky

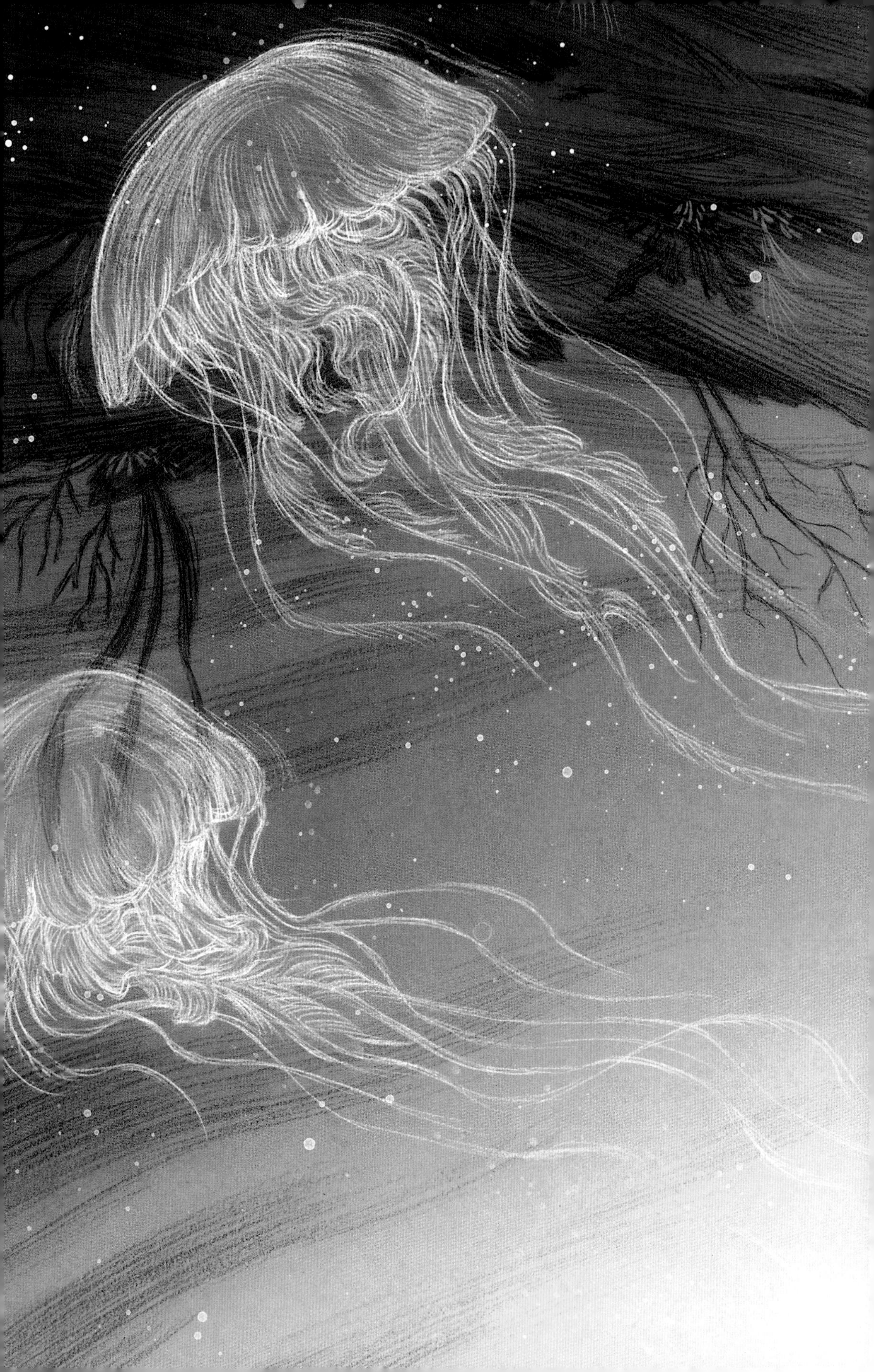

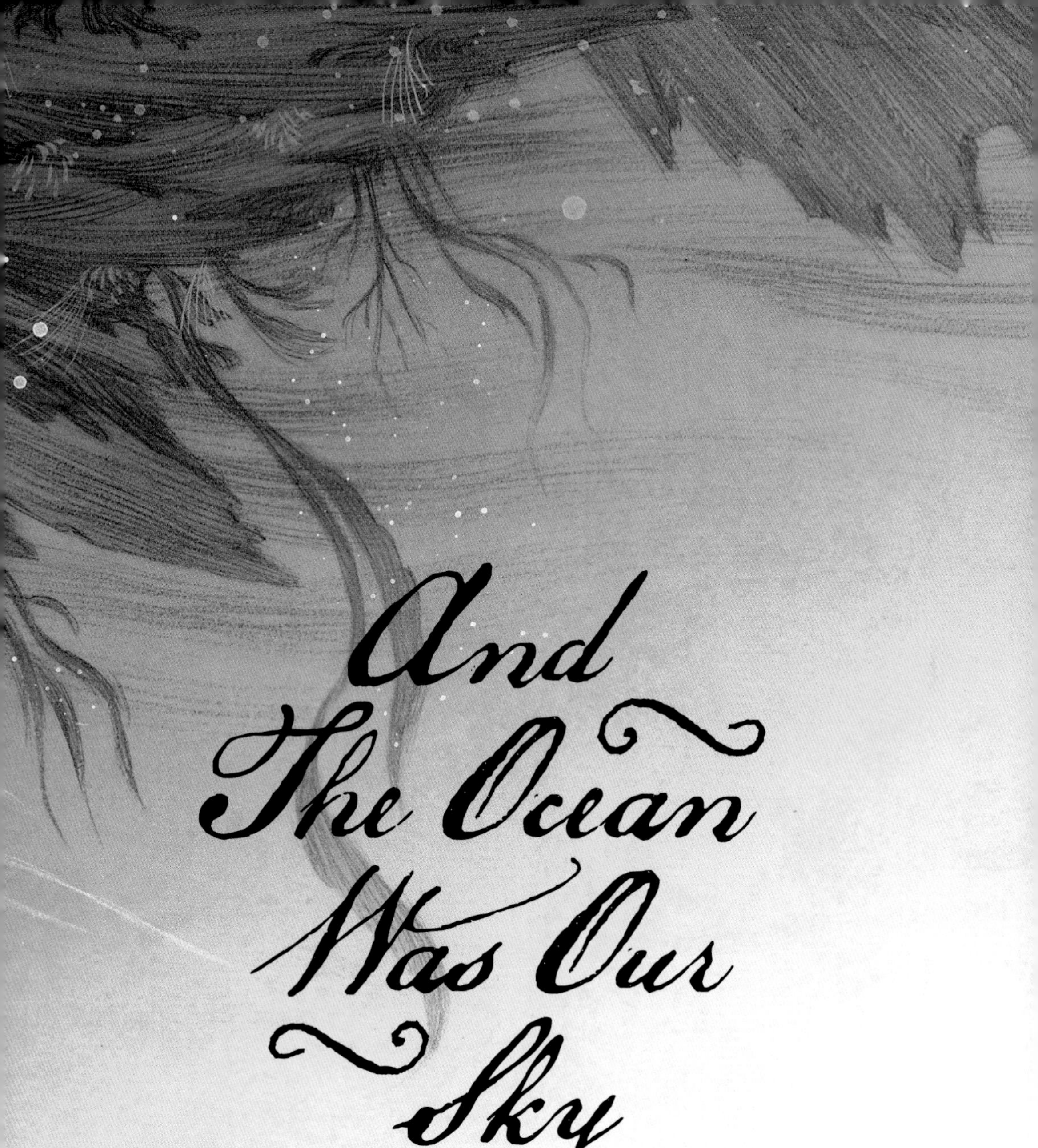

And The Ocean Was Our Sky

Patrick Ness

illustrated by Rovina Cai

HARPER TEEN

An Imprint of HarperCollins*Publishers*

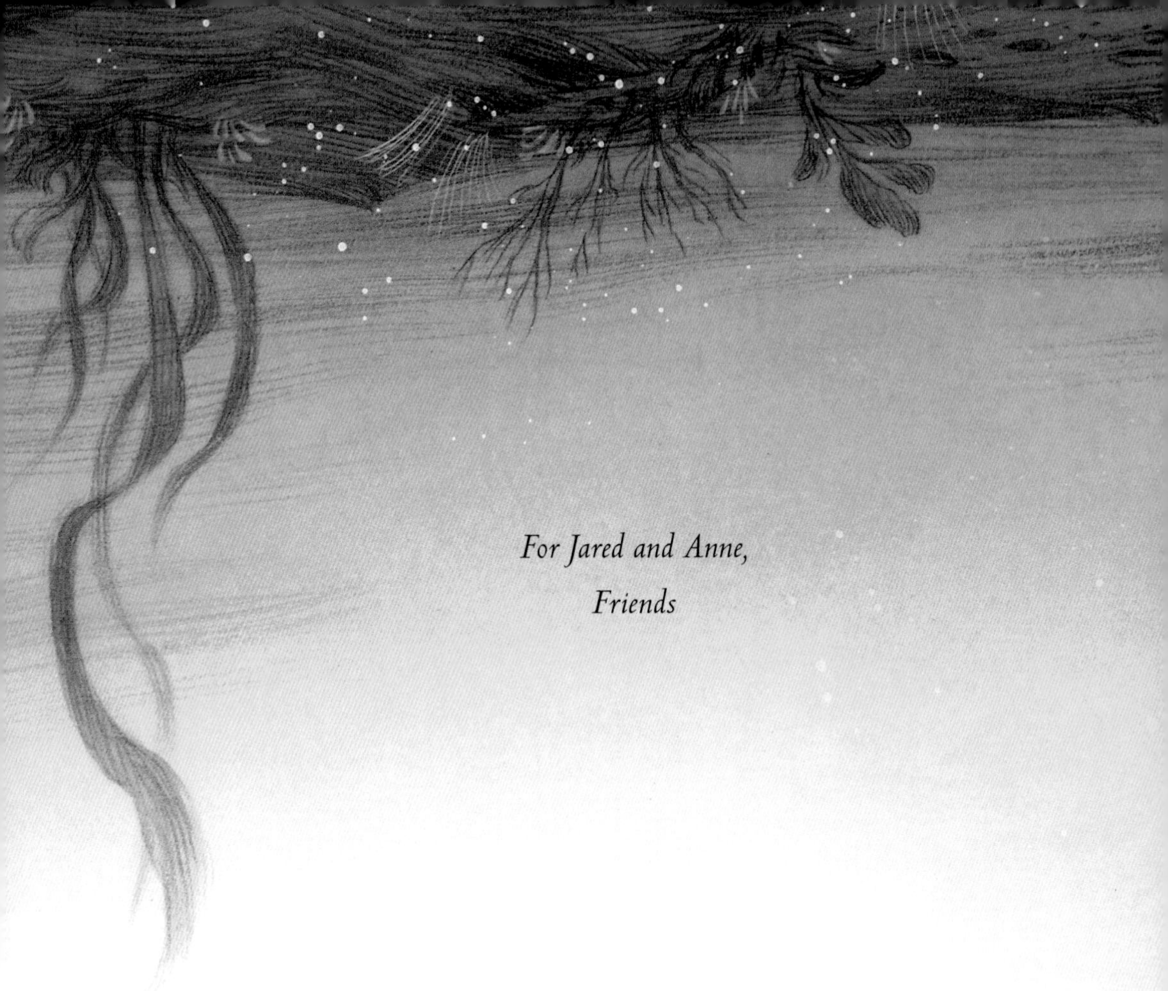

For Jared and Anne,

Friends

HarperTeen is an imprint of HarperCollins Publishers.

And The Ocean Was Our Sky

For information address HarperCollins Children's Books, a division of HarperCollins Publishers, 195 Broadway, New York, NY 10007.
www.epicreads.com
Library of Congress Control Number: 2018938254
ISBN 978-0-06-286072-9 (hardcover)
ISBN 978-0-06-287744-4 (international edition)
18 19 20 21 22 SCP 10 9 8 7 6 5 4 3 2 1
❖
First Edition

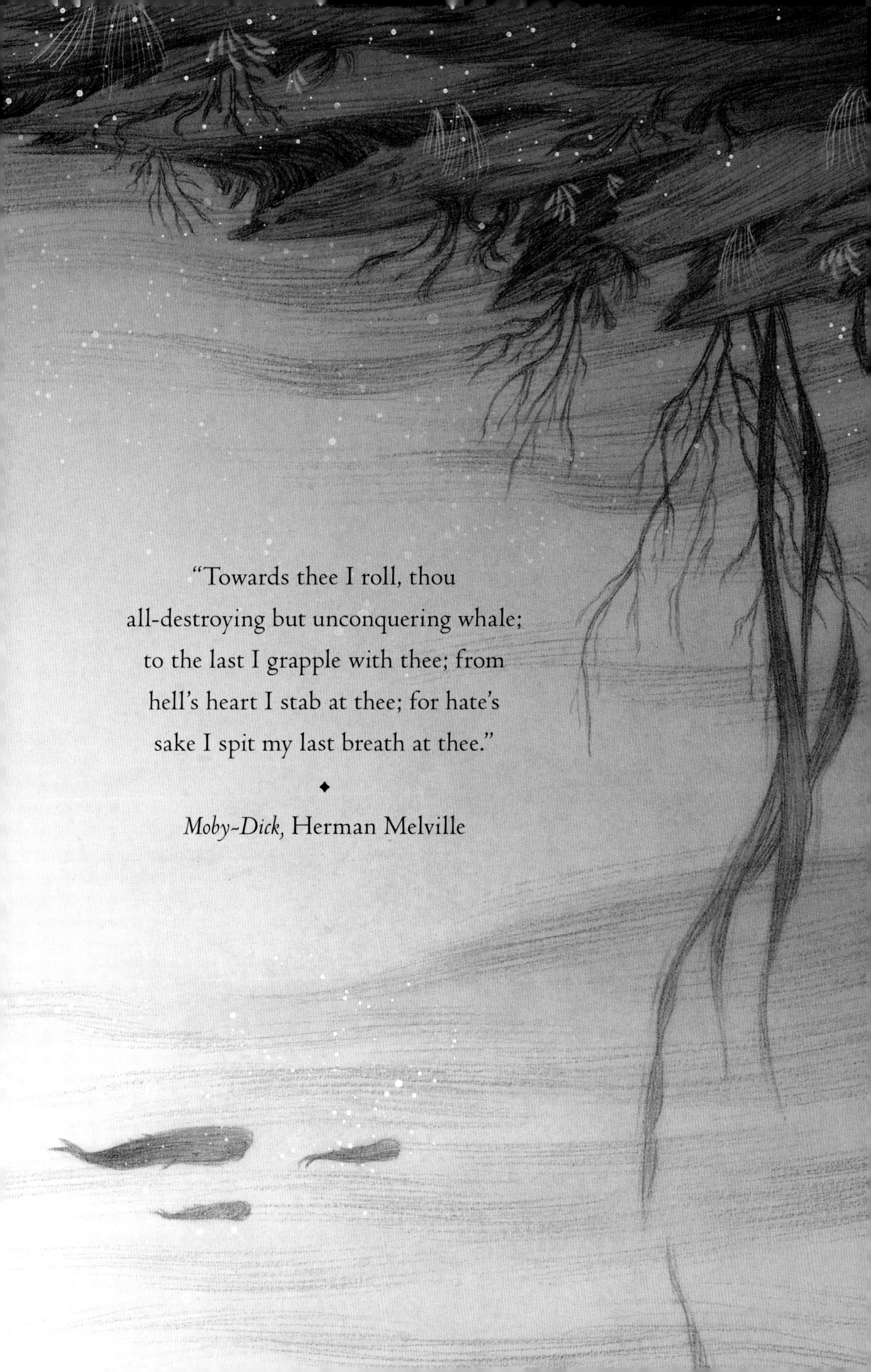

"Towards thee I roll, thou
all-destroying but unconquering whale;
to the last I grapple with thee; from
hell's heart I stab at thee; for hate's
sake I spit my last breath at thee."

◆

Moby-Dick, Herman Melville

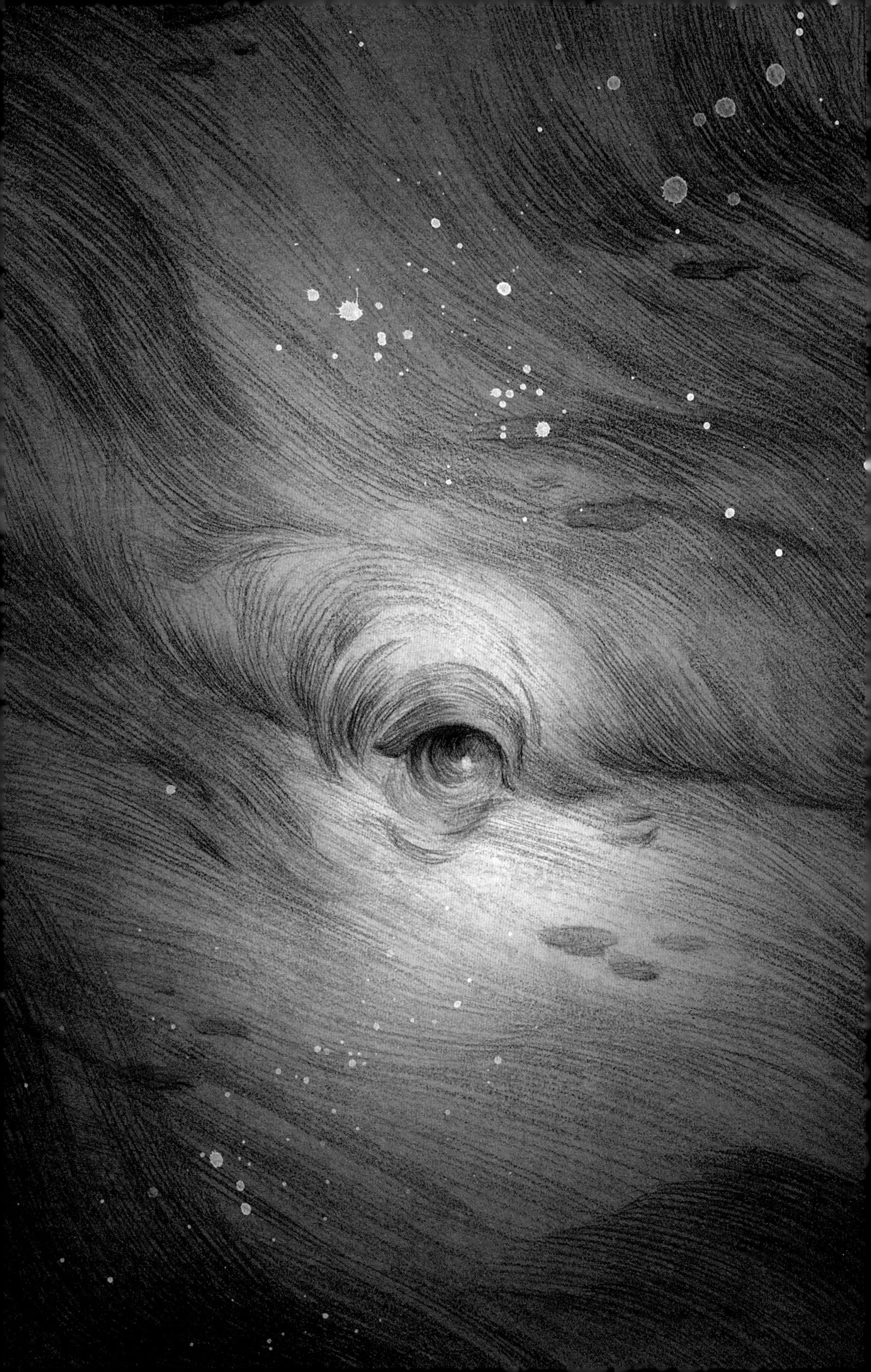

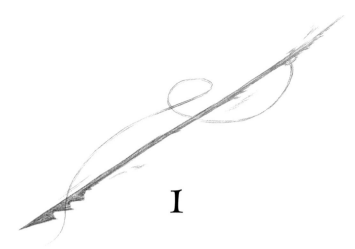

I

Call me Bathsheba.

It is not my name, but the name I use for this story. A name, I hoped, that would be free of prophecy, free of the burden of a future placed upon it, free of any destiny that would tear it from my hands and destroy worlds.

You think I overstate. You are wrong.

We are a people of prophecy, and when I was a child and still a stupid calf, ignorant of all beyond the reaches of our own stretch of sea, my grandmother had said, simply, "You will hunt."

It carried the weight of prophecy.

"But we are not hunters," my mother had replied with the fearful bafflement that was her regular face to my grandmother. "We do not hunt. We have never hunted." Her voice took on a hopeful and hopeless tone, the one that used to irritate me into fury but the memory of which now breaks my heart quite in half. "Unless you mean the small hunts," my mother said, hopelessly hopeful, "the ones that every family must—"

"I do not," said my grandmother.

She did not.

And everything I might have been, the different futures I might have taken, all my different lives and deaths that existed in their endless possibilities were extinguished in a single repetition of her three words. "You will hunt."

Was it prediction? Had she had a proper vision? Or was it a command, as it so often feels in the case of the prophetic? When you predict the future, when you do so strongly and you cling to it, how much of that future do you then cause to happen?

These are questions that haunt me.

At the time, though, they weren't allowed to matter, for into training I immediately went — my mother never strong enough to overrule my grandmother — into the schools and the vocationals, into a new way of life until, at sixteen, the age of Apprenticeship, there I was, where this story begins: harpoons strapped to my back, swimming along the decks of the great hunting ship *Alexandra*, our sails catching the currents, the Abyss below us, the ocean our sky.

And all that might have been was long, long gone.

For I, a lowly but eager Third Apprentice, was about to

begin the final hunt that ever was. The hunt for a legend, a myth, a devil.

Pray for our souls.

Because this is the story of how we found him. ◆

2

"LOOK SHARP," SAID CAPTAIN ALEXANDRA. As is traditional, our ship bore her name, much like her body bore most of the *ship*, the ropes from the bow tied to her fins, broad as any three of my young shipmates. The Captain pulls her ship, as is right, as is proper.

We sailed silently over the Abyss. I was Watch Left, swimming above and to the side of our Captain, matched further out front by First Apprentice Treasure and to the side by Second Apprentice Wilhelmina, "Willem," Watch Right. We scanned the surface of the Abyss below us, its sun shining from underneath, like sailing across boiling light.

Behind us, on the *Alexandra*, our sailors made ready. The Captain was sure we were close to a prize. She could smell it, she said, and though this seemed improbable, we had learned in the months of this voyage not to doubt her.

Never to doubt her. Captain Alexandra was both famous and infamous, little of it for good reason past her success at the hunt. Everyone knew about the short, rusted end of a man's harpoon still sticking from her great head. She was the Captain who'd survived, the Captain who even though the harpoon must, on some level, impede her echolocation, nevertheless persisted, thrived, became the one thing that everyone, *everyone*, was sure about Captain Alexandra: she was the best hunter in the sea.

"Something approaches," she said, eyes forward, great tail increasing its kick. "Something rises."

"Where?" whispered Willem to my right, desperately searching the white froth below us.

"Quiet," Treasure said back. She was senior Apprentice. How often do you suppose she let us forget that?

The water filled with the clicks of our echolocations. The Captain left us to it, trusting her sense of smell, her eyes, her clairvoyance, for all I knew.

"Less than a league," Treasure said. "Center right."

"Look sharp," the Captain said again.

"Yes," Willem answered. "Yes, I've located it."

"And our Bathsheba?" the Captain asked, not looking back.

For I had remained silent. I had not located it yet.

I furiously sent out my clicks, waiting for the responses to echo off the great ball of waxy liquid in my forehead. I heard nothing from the center right, from where Treasure and Willem were claiming such certainty. I clicked again, and nothing. All I sensed there was empty ocean. I was the newest Apprentice, barely a year into our hunt, but I was not incompetent. And though my anxiety was growing, I also began to suspect Treasure and Willem were lying to impress their Captain, perhaps falling into one of the traps that even I knew she occasionally set for unwary Apprentices.

"Bathsheba?" the Captain asked again, her voice somehow both playful and menacing, as if I were prey kept alive only at the whim of its predator.

I clicked. Again, and nothing. Again, and—

I turned sharply left. "Not center right," I said, surprised even at myself. I clicked once more. I was nervous. But I was sure. "Third of a league. Left and left again."

"No—" started Treasure.

"Is it?" said Willem.

"Quite so, our Bathsheba," said the Captain, surging forward, pulling the great ship behind us to the left and a notch left again.

"I've found it!" Treasure said, too loud because too late.

"It rises," said the Captain. And the hunt was on. ◆

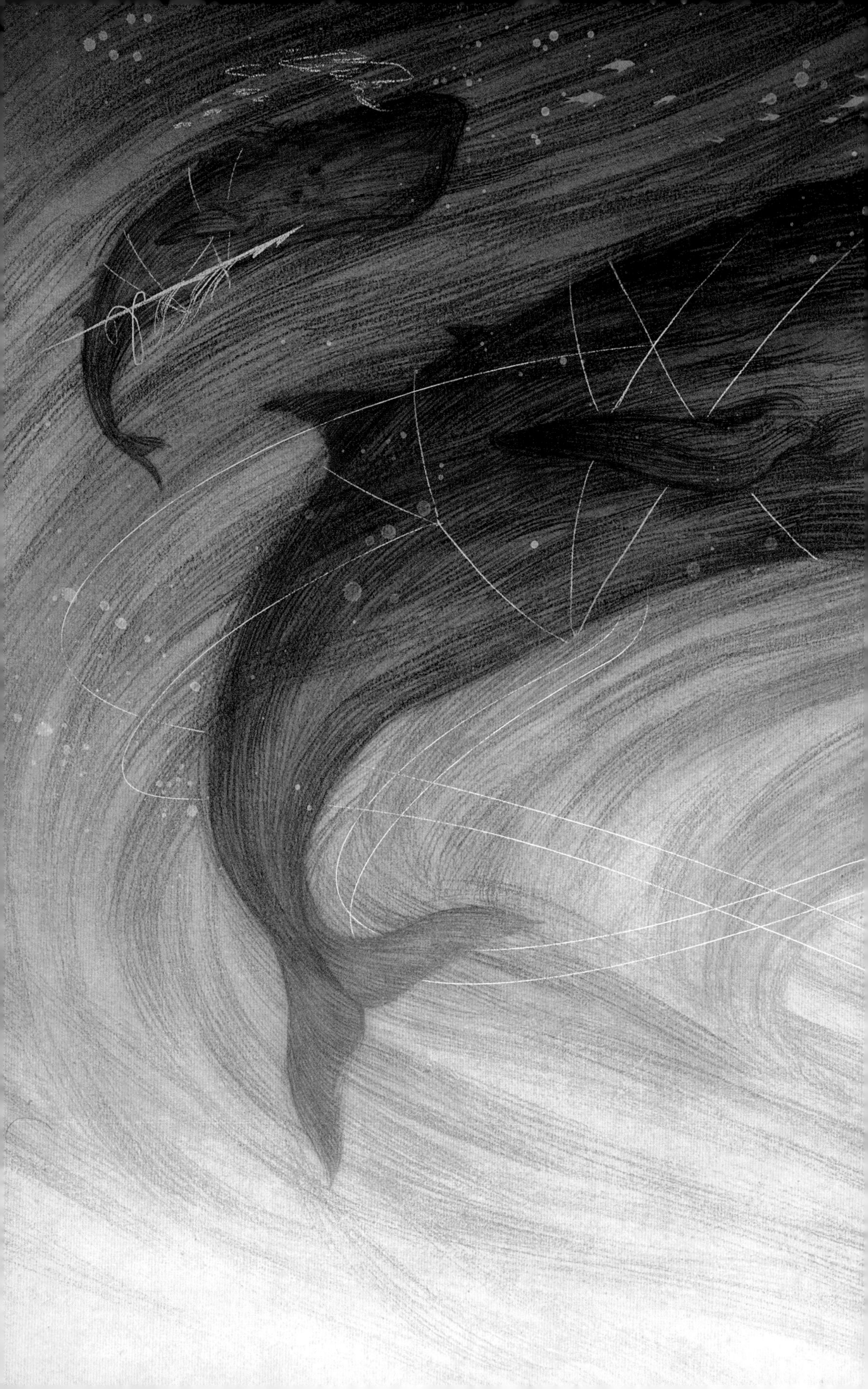

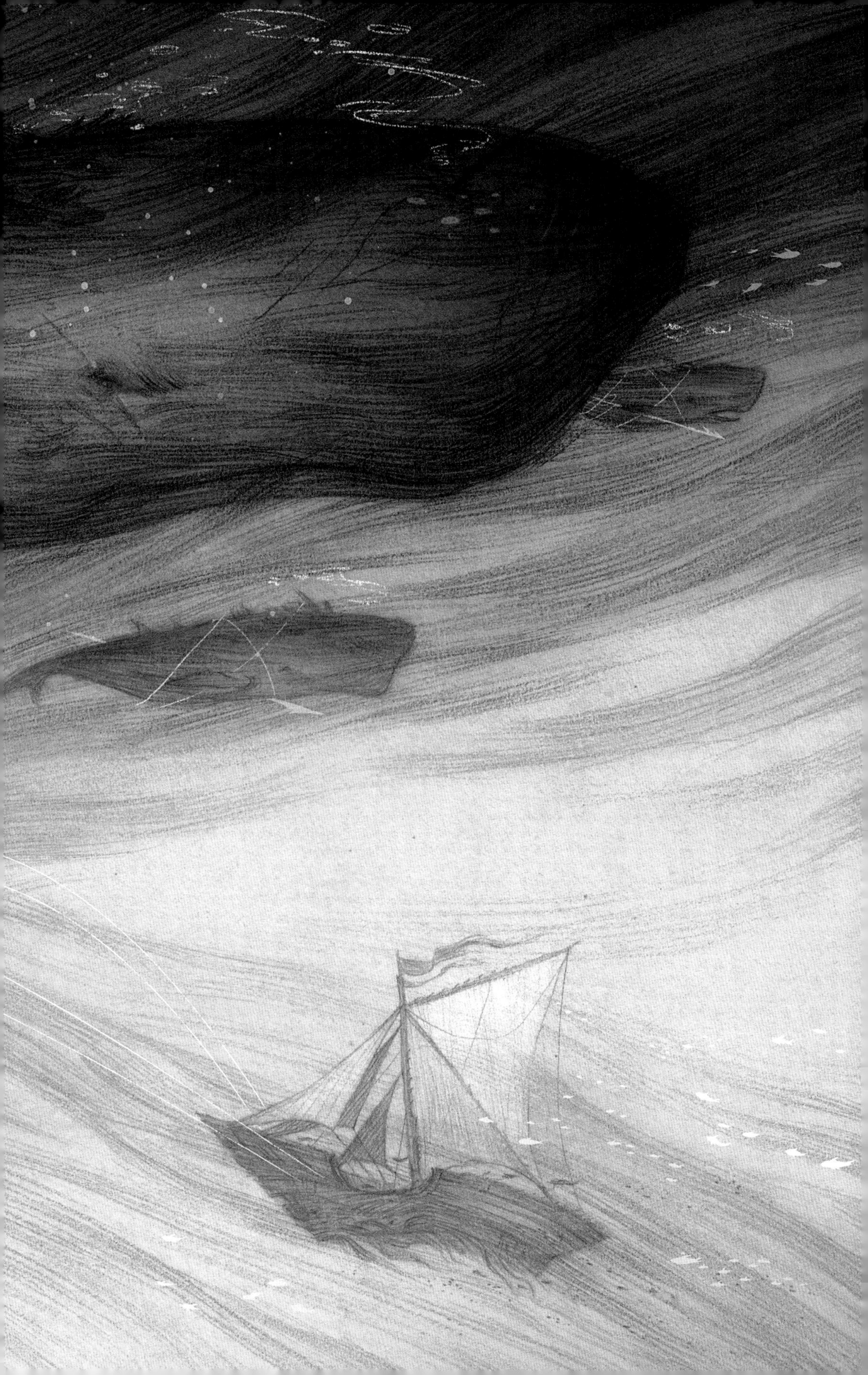

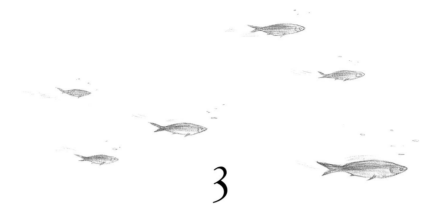

3

LET ME BE CLEAR, RIGHT FROM THE START. I hate the hunt, but I loved it then. Now, of course, after all that occurred, after all are dead, after I waited for a rescue that might never come, no one would blame me for hating it.

(Though there are always eager whispers from others, even now, a look of excitement in an eye, a hesitant suggestion that I might perhaps recount my story yet again for the thrill of it. Whose thrill? Not mine.)

(I have discussed this with soldiers and they have confirmed to me that, yes, there are those who romance the hunt the way they romance war; in their safety, they imagine heroism, they imagine a place in history, an invisible pride that won't feed their children but will raise them above their neighbors; they never imagine the despair; they never imagine the blood and suffering; they never imagine how your heart dies and dies again; I, like nearly every soldier before our wars finally stopped, have taken refuge in a silence so firm it is only the most witless who dare intrude upon it.)

But now, here, once and for all, I set down my tale. I am not who I was then. I said I was ignorant, and I am not wrong, though by that point I *had* learned that men lived upside down from us, that for them the ocean was below, the Abyss above, our gravities only meeting at the surface. I knew, too, that our writers speculated about worlds where whales also lived this way around, rising up to meet men rather than swimming down to them, but to us, this was nearly blasphemy, a fantasy of men pretending to a dominance they'd never have.

I had learned of our pasts, too, how the hunts between whale and man had gone on for thousands of years, as our societies reflected each other, grew together, war driving both to further and further innovations.

I had learned, in short, to love the hunt, not merely for itself, but for its history, for its part in my identity. And I did love it. I had my own, personal reasons by that point, too, but what more reason did a young whale need than the fact that men had hunted us for time immemorial and hunting men was what we did in return? It was a whale's duty, if so prophesied, and I embraced it.

But that was then. If you hear what I say and still wish yourself there, wish yourself a hero, wish yourself a hunter, then either I have failed in my telling or you are a fool. ◆

4

WE CLOSED THE THIRD OF A LEAGUE IN moments. This was my favorite part: the thrill of the chase. The water rushing past us, swimming at full speed, the mighty sails of our ship — tended with skill by our six-strong crew of sailors who'd been at sea longer than I had been alive — catching the current to add to the speed with which our Captain pulled. Everything a rush, everything a push, everything full of intent and purpose, the sun below dazzling up with shafts of spinning light.

The world, alive.

"Ready harpoons," the Captain said, and we three Apprentices did so, maneuvering them with fin-flicks on the webbing strapped to our sides, settling the weapons into the coiled launchers held tight against our breasts. Our technology was then so advanced it would require only a flexing of a muscle near the pectoral fin to fire them.

"We should be able to see it," Treasure said. "Any second now."

"Truly?" said our Captain. "Is it not a league away to the center right?"

That, at least, shut Treasure up. It was a mistake to ever assume our Captain did not notice something or that she would forget it.

But we *were* close. The path favored my side, and my clicks raced forward and back with increasing frequency. We still could not yet see it, the surface of the Abyss growing choppier, foamier, obscuring what our eyes could discern.

"Ready nets!" our Captain called back to the ship. The sailors had guessed their Captain's intent, and nets were ready for casting. We would harpoon our prey to either death or incipient mortality, and the sailors would bring in the carcasses. Every bit of the prey would be used, their bones for tallow and soaps, their skin for sails, their meat – inedible to us – as bait for the vast shoals of prey who, once attracted, we could eat at our leisure.

Mostly, though, in that paradox of all wars, we hunted to prevent from being hunted, just as they did.

"There!" Willem called.

And there it was, bobbing up in the foam of the Abyss—

The bowed hull of a man ship. ◆

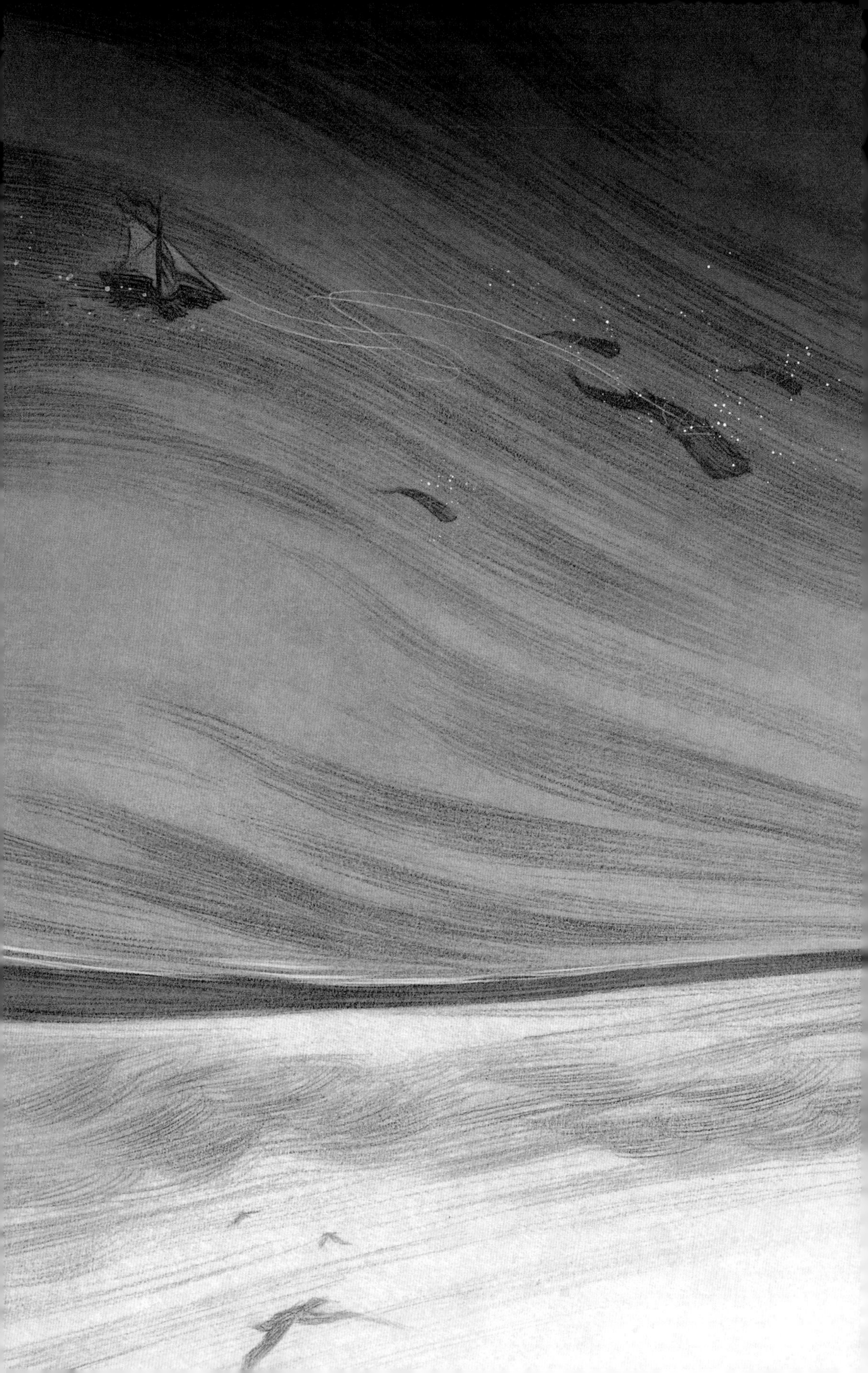

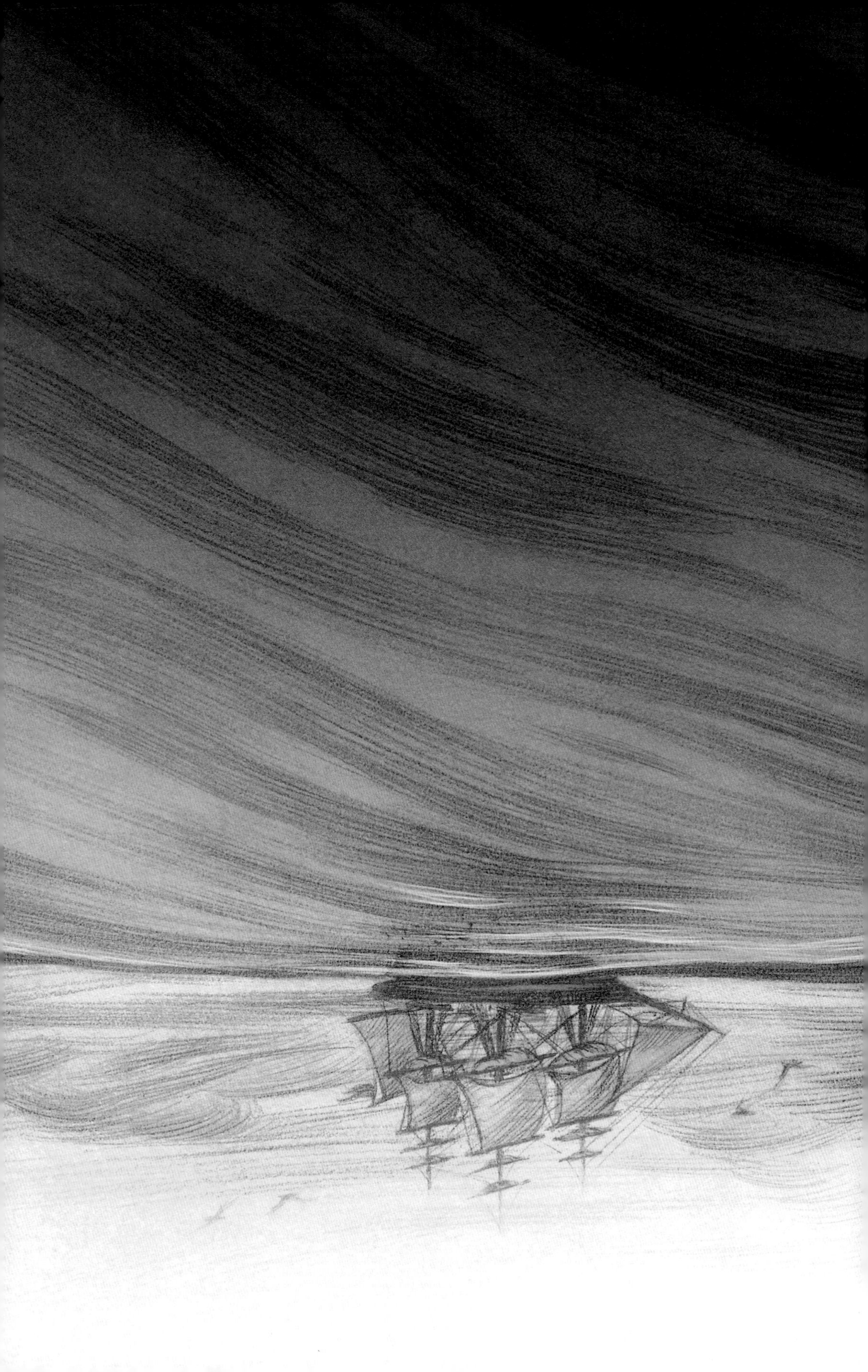

5

The Captain swooped suddenly left, veering into my path. I corrected only just in time.

"Sharper than that!" she snapped as she swam past, fast as a spear. I swam furiously to keep up, cursing my stupidity. For a fully hulled ship, we always circled first to see its strengths, to see with what weight it bobbed up from the Abyss, where its weaknesses might be, though they were always the same: the great sides, slatted and curved. Hard, but not hard enough to withstand the battering of the great head of a Captain, should she choose.

She frequently chose.

A ship like this would be easy prey. Small risk, but potentially great reward. I readied to join her in the attack that would be called for in seconds—

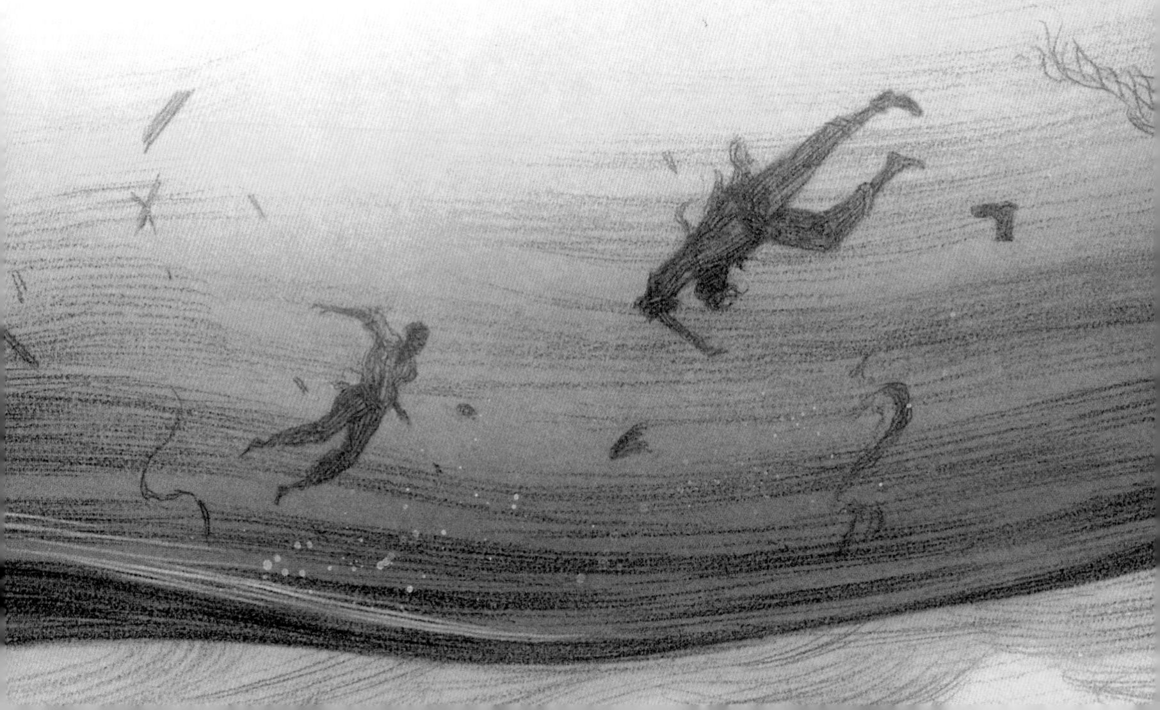

"There are men in the water!" called Treasure.

"*Dead* men," Willem said, wonderingly, and indeed, as the foam cleared here and there, I saw we were swimming above corpses. Their faces were upturned from the Abyss into the water, something men only did when they drowned. They had not yet mastered the breather bubble, currently resting in the throats of every one of our people, an invention that liberated us almost entirely from the need to turn downward into the Abyss to breathe, an evolutionary calamity we resented, but one that did have other benefits – oxygen to fuel our warm-blooded veins, hearts that pumped rich blood to the brains that had led us to dominate the ocean.

We were whales, independent and fierce.

(But there is an "almost" lurking in my words above, and

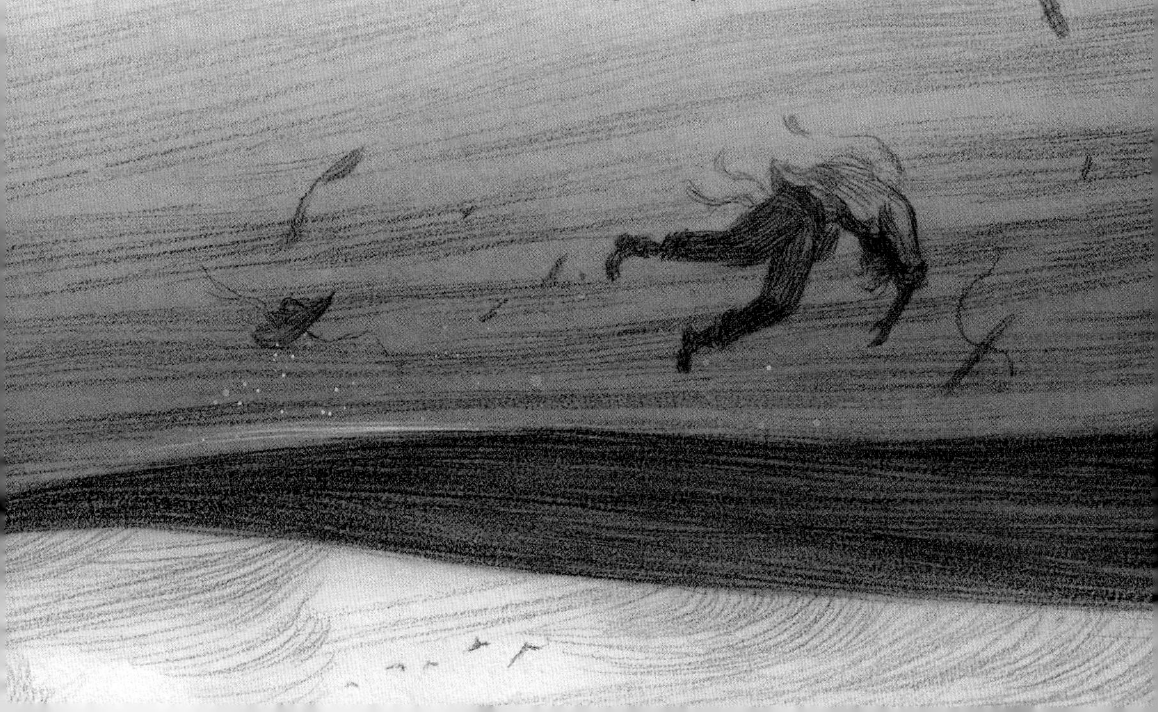

on that "almost" yet hangs an entire destiny. For we *do* still have to occasionally breathe in the world of men. Which means men must be reckoned with, one way or another.)

"What happened here?" Treasure asked, and it was a fair question. The man ship seemed intact, but its crew littered the surface, a blanket of them slowly forming itself, yanked apart here and there by sharks.

The Captain ignored Treasure's question, accelerating ahead, loosing herself from the ropes that tied her to the *Alexandra*. "Collect the bodies," she said to the sailors, who set to work. "There may be another pod nearby."

"There's another pod?" Willem said, looking around as she swam. In regular circumstances, other pods could be friend or foe. When prey was in the water, they were only foe.

Free of the ship, the Captain moved with a speed it was an effort to keep up with, though she was three times our size at the very least. Silently, she circled the man ship. Then again. We kept back, following her from a height, rising above the Abyss to let our sailors do their work. As is traditional, our sailors were a smaller species of whale than us. A class all on their own, secretive, indispensable. They bit the heads off the men first, tumbling them into a separate net — men's teeth were valuable as a fake digestive aid and fetched a high price among the gullible rich. The bodies would be broken down when the hunt was over, our sailors working long into the night, boiling, scrubbing, churning.

"There is something . . ." the Captain said, pulling herself to a stop after a third silent circle. "Bathsheba!" She called me to her side with an unignorable command. "What's there?"

Wondering, as I always did, what our Captain saw in her own echolocation, how much the rusted harpoon impaired it, I sent out my own waves of sound at the hull. It was smooth, the same curves that men always made to cut the water, not *so* very different from the water-slicing shapes of *our* ships, though ours were flatter and more open to accommodate our superior size. We used masts and sails like men, too, to catch the currents. Or should I say, men used them like we did?

Still, this man ship was nothing special. A thin blanket of barnacles across the hull, as to be expected, but nothing—

Click.

"Yes," said the Captain, swimming warily. "Investigate."

I looked at Treasure and Willem, both a distance away, both as shocked as I was that the order was for me.

"Do not make me command you again," the Captain said.

I had no choice. I swam to the hull. ◆

23

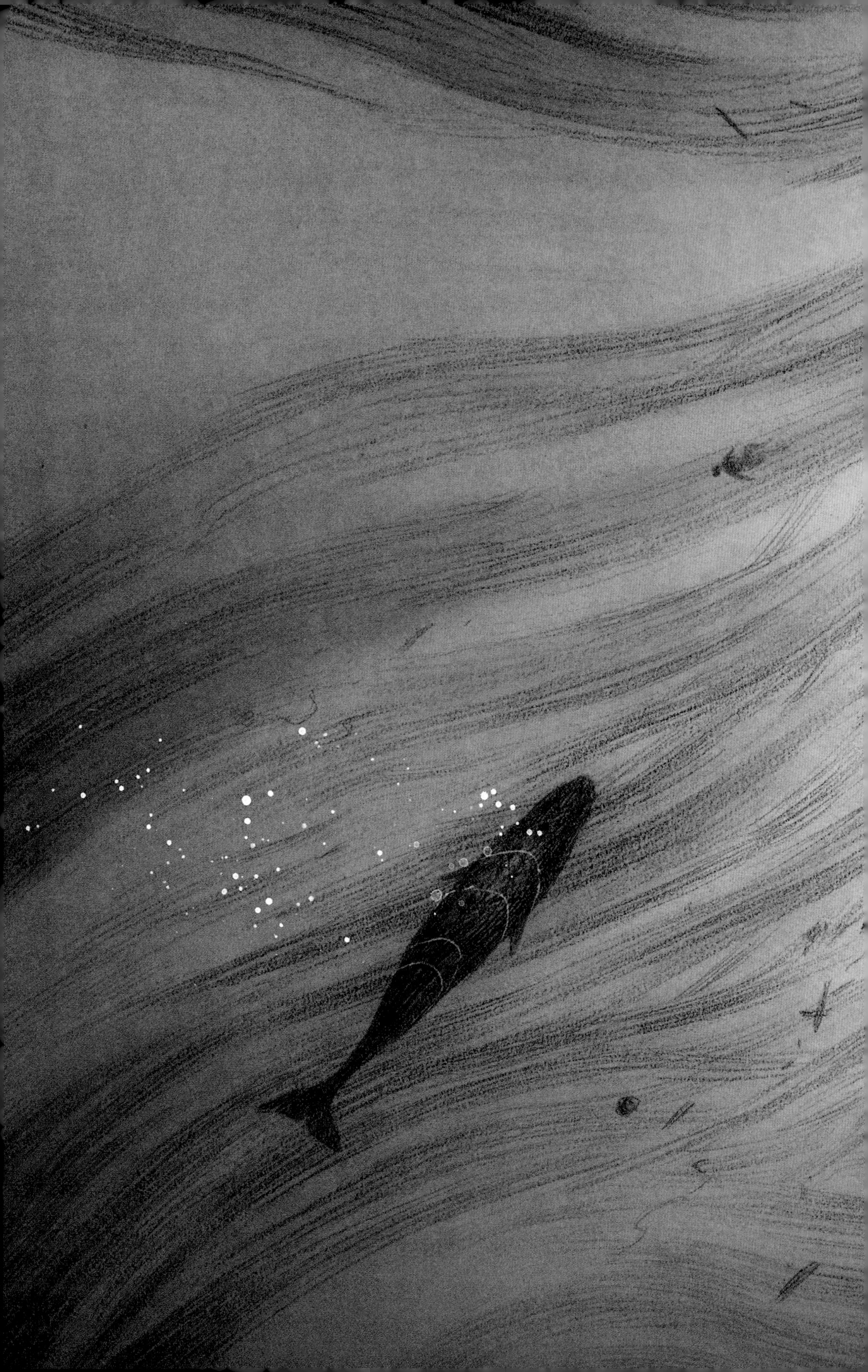

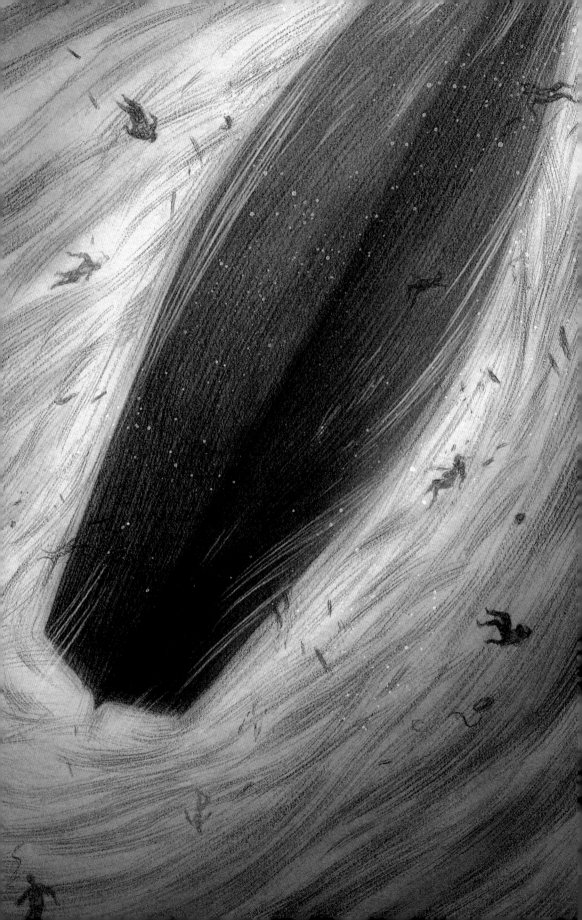

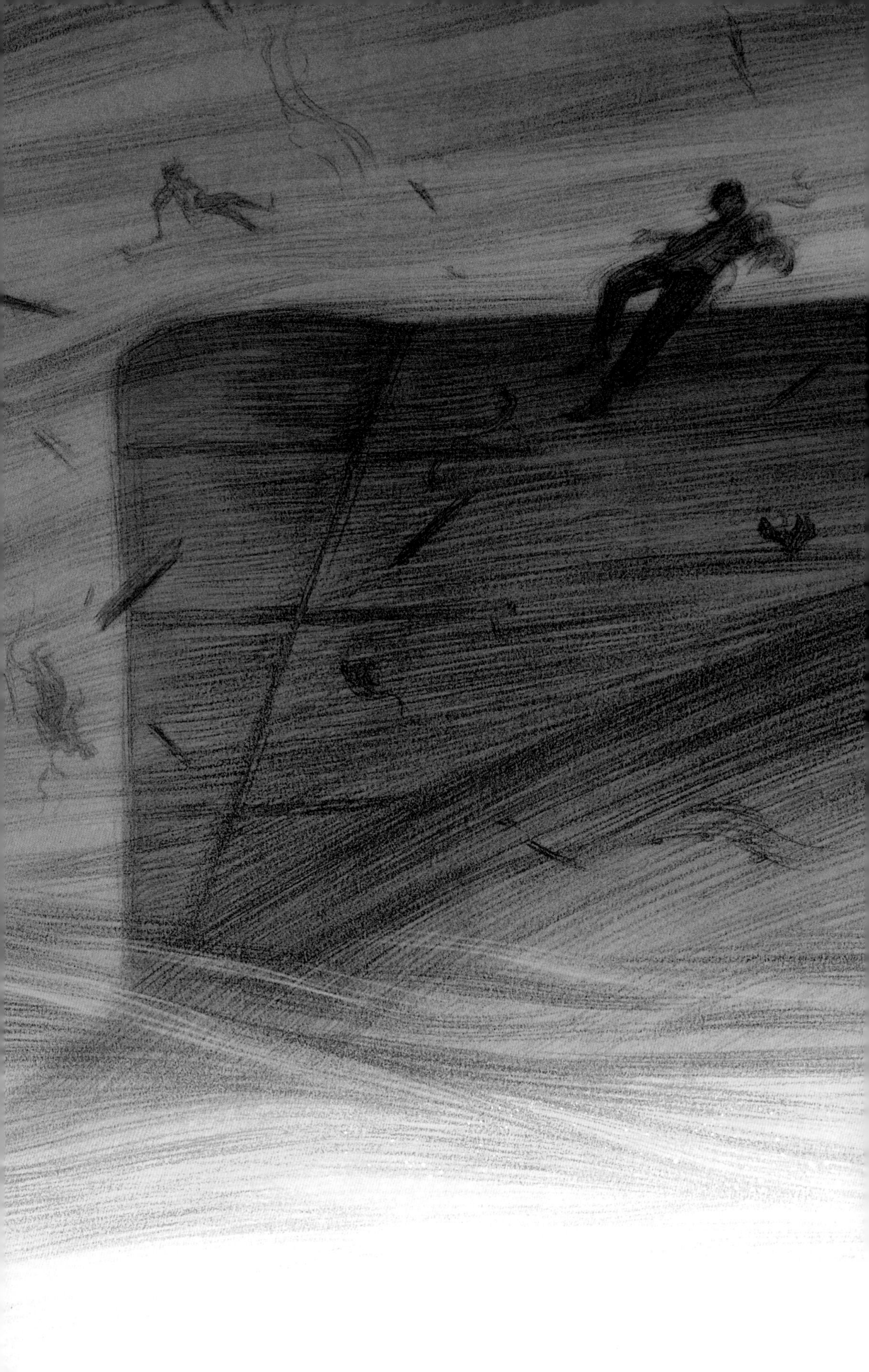

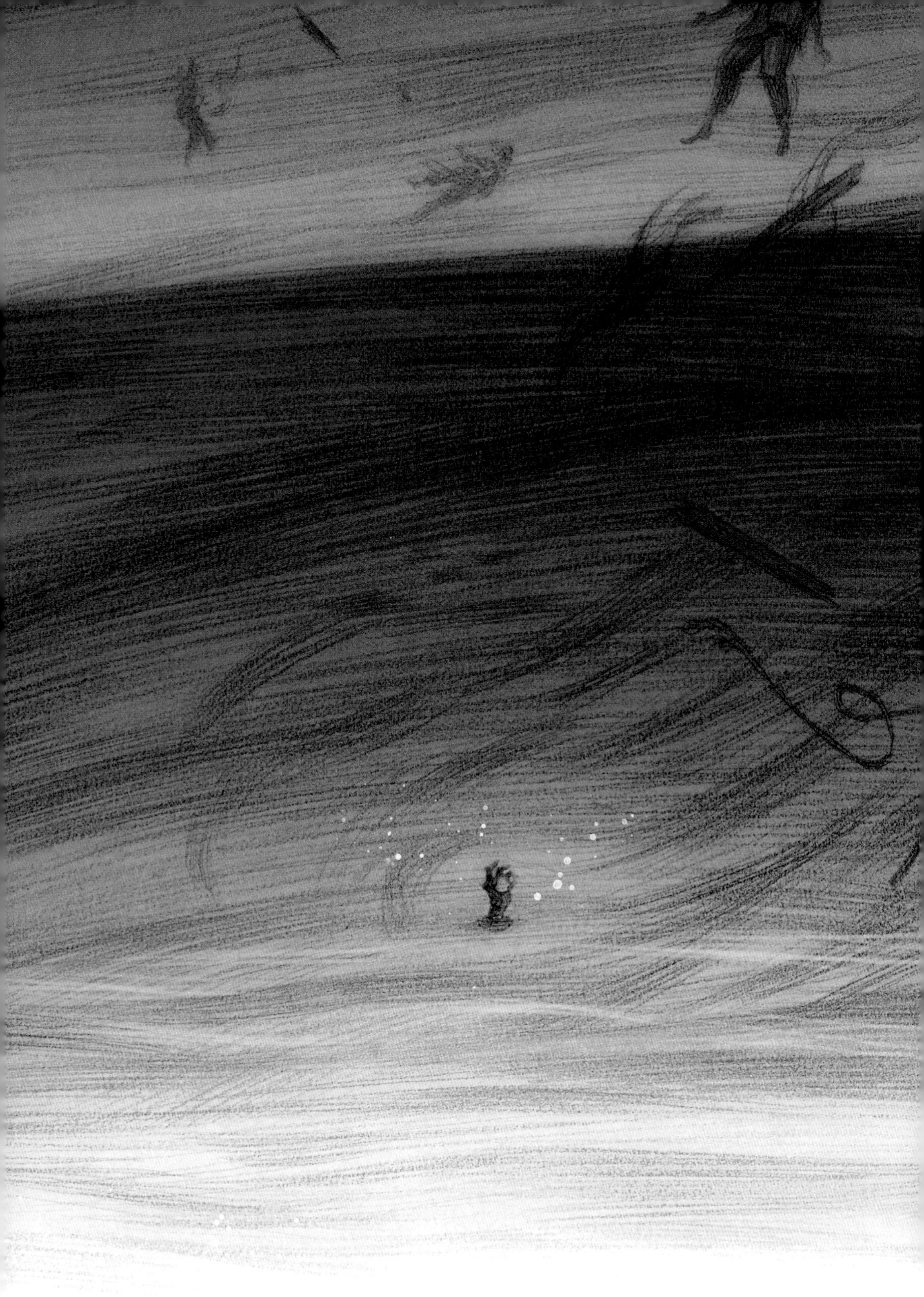

6

WHAT I FOUND WAS THAT MOST CURIOUS of all the odd questions of men, the one that had sparked debate over so very many generations. We knew from our own skeletons that the bones existed in our fins, but there was still distaste for how *naked* they seemed on man: the starlike spindle they used to such advantage; that allowed them to make more elaborate boats than ours, despite their

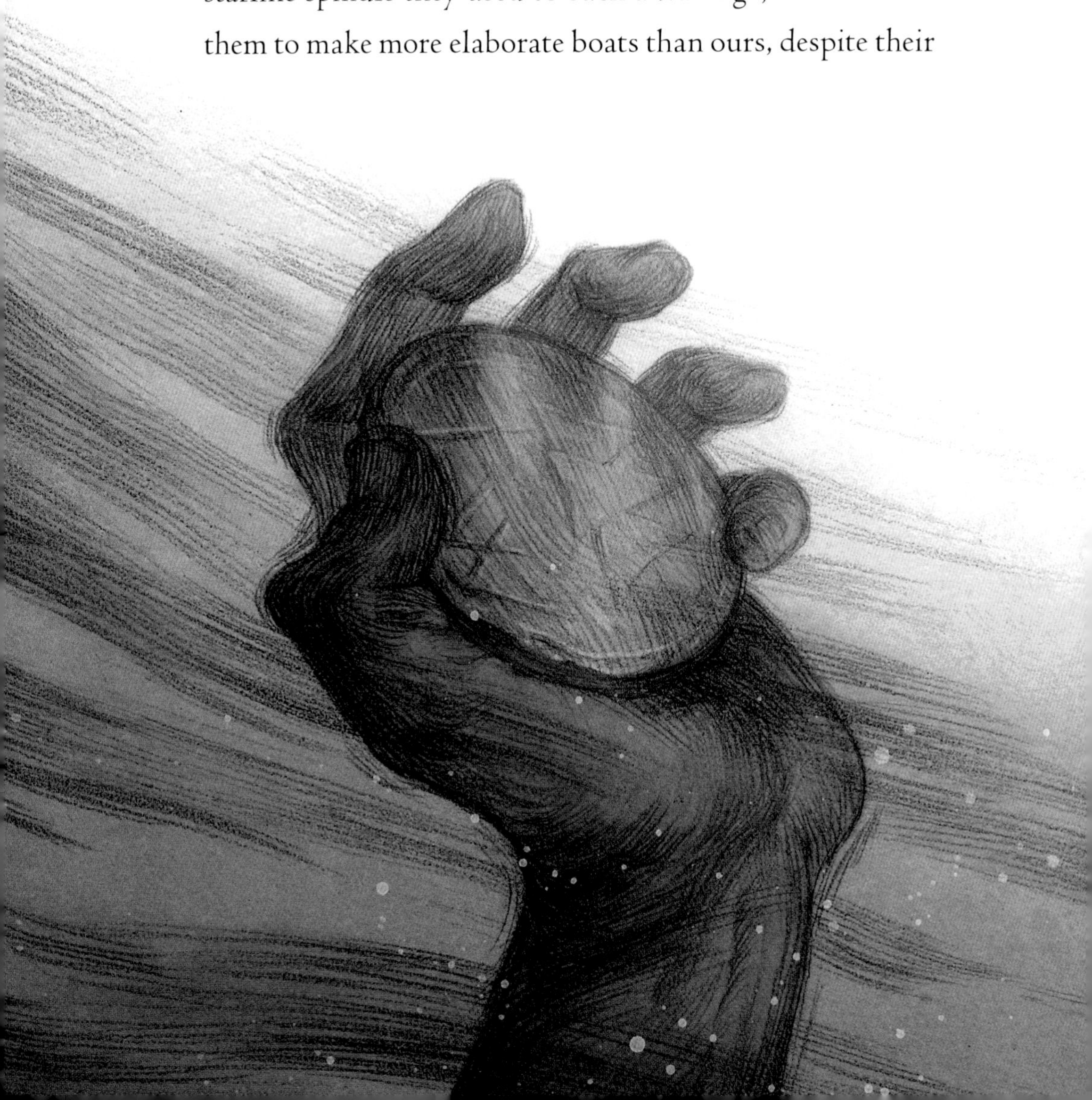

utter primitivism; that allowed them to weave their body coverings, another art we had only learned as a spoil of hunting them, though our historians were already beginning to erase this fact and claim we'd invented weaving ourselves.

All because, in place of a fin, they had a hand.

For that was what was sticking out of the hull of the boat. I mean these words as I speak them. A hand, sticking out of what could only be a watertight hole cut purposely into the hull.

A hand sticking out into the naked ocean.

And it was grasping something. ◆

7

"THERE'S A MAN CONNECTED TO THIS?" Willem asked, as we all regarded the hand.

"Don't be a fool," Treasure said. "It is surely a trick."

"But what kind of trick?" I said. "The ship is wrecked. Its crew is dead."

"But who wrecked it?" Willem asked. "And who killed the men?"

"Cease this idiotic chatter," the Captain barked. "It is a message."

"A message?" Willem asked.

The Captain spun sharply, striking Willem hard across the head with her tail fin, sending her spinning up into water, a spiral of blood following her. The Captain turned to me. "What does it hold, Bathsheba? What's in the hand?"

I swam down close, aware of the huge tail that could easily send *me* spinning. I secretly felt Willem was right in her confused wariness. My initial question hadn't been answered. We hunted ships, ones with living hunters aboard. Occasionally, we'd find one wrecked and picked clean by another hunting pod, but in the year I had swam as Apprentice under Captain Alexandra, we'd never come across one simply dead in the water. Men were barbarous, of course, everyone knew it. But *would* they kill each other like this? Would they cripple their own ship in the middle of the ocean?

I could feel my heartbeat pulsing in my head, a thump of nerves I tried to calm as I turned my left eye to the hand, getting close enough for it to reach me, should it want to. Though, surely, the owner of the hand must be dead. Mustn't he?

The hand held out a disc only slightly smaller than itself, as if presenting it.

But presenting it to whom?

"It is round," I said. "Gold."

"A coin?" suggested Treasure.

"More," the Captain demanded. "Tell me more."

"There are symbols on it," I said. "Three upward triangles. Perhaps mountains?"

"I did not ask for analysis, I asked for description."

"A cross-mark along the bottom," I swiftly added. "A crooked line next to it."

The Captain was silent. Then she spoke only a single word, "Move," and she was already swimming to a distance to start her run. I sped away from the ship as fast as I could, and even then she only just missed me as she slammed into the hull, so violently the ship cracked right in two. After such power, she seemed to merely shrug the rest of the ship to pieces.

The wood surrounding the hand floated free, revealing the young, terrified, very much alive man it belonged to, still grasping the disc, shackled to a board from the hull that was now dragging him to his death.

We watched him drown for a moment before the Captain astonished us by issuing a breather bubble from her blowhole that surrounded the young man's head, giving him air.

"Captain?" I asked, shocked.

"The lines you described at the bottom are not symbols," she said, circling the man in the water as he struggled to the surface of the Abyss. A simple push of her tail was enough to tumble him back toward us. "They are letters in man language. T and W."

Willem returned, swimming close to me as this sunk in. Even Treasure swam near, we three Apprentices bound in fright at what our Captain was suggesting.

Until it moved past suggestion into fact.

"We have found," the Captain said, "the trail of Toby Wick." ◆

8

EVEN BY THAT POINT, EVEN THAT EARLY ON, I had already killed many men, but I had tried to avoid this destiny.

Though I was never asked my own feelings about my grandmother's prophecy that I would hunt, I had accepted it with a hardness the younger me would have wrongly called maturity. Like all whales, I hated men, and with good reason: their bloody killings, their sloppy, wasteful harvesting proving that they killed as much for sport as for need. They purported to dominate the sea while being able to stick only to the under-surface of the Abyss, threatening our great pods and cities from its margins.

I hunted because our cities needed hunters. And as I've said, by the time I reached my Apprenticeship, I had my own reasons, too. But even as my grandmother prophesied my fate those years before, my willingness still contained one small rebuke. There was one part of the hunt, the unspoken part, the superstitious part, that I would not join in. My mother and grandmother had raised me to be what my grandmother *was* and what she'd hoped my mother would be.

"I cannot *only* be a hunter," I said. "I am also a thinker. I will not join their religion."

"You will," my grandmother said, making it both command and inevitability.

"I will *not*. Fools and brutes, suffocating on superstition, worshipping their devil–"

"Do not say his name," my mother suddenly joined in. "Do not speak it."

"Why?" I taunted. "Bad luck? The devil will come to find you if you speak his name aloud?"

This, I must admit, was the bravado of youth, proclaiming separation from my old-fashioned elders. But I was more prescient than I knew.

"I will hunt, but I will not be a fool."

"Daughter of mine, do not say it."

But I did.

"Toby Wick," I said. More than once, perhaps even relishing the pain on my mother's face, the distaste on my grandmother's. I named our devil. Our monster. Our myth.

But who is the fool? I said his name, and now I had found him. ◆

9

THE YOUNG MALE BECAME OUR PRISONER, though in his first panic, he nearly drowned. The bubble breather is a reservoir of air we developed from a chemical in flatfish that extends oxygen use and another we discovered in coral that helps the bubble keep its shape. Even so, it's a shock to take a first breath while still underwater.

I wouldn't have even been sure a man could master it, if I had ever thought of such a ridiculous notion. This one, at least, was struggling.

"Where is he?" our Captain demanded of him, her tongue thick with the language of men, one all hunters learn though it is stupendously difficult.

The young male was surprised, to say the least, to hear a great Captain of a whale, fifty times his size, five hundred times his weight, speak in his own language, though the words stretched as they traveled across water rather than air. He struggled again against his breather, swallowing water, coughing, swallowing more, not knowing which way was up in this space he was never meant to live. Honestly, how did these creatures ever think they were fit to sail upon the great ocean?

"Take him to the surface," the Captain said to me.

I was startled. "The surface?"

She rounded on me. "Have we become a crew where the Captain must issue every order twice? *Take him to the surface.*"

I needed no further reminder. I took the terrified young man in my mouth — which only terrified him more — and swam to the surface of the Abyss, rolling upside down to enter the world of men. ◆

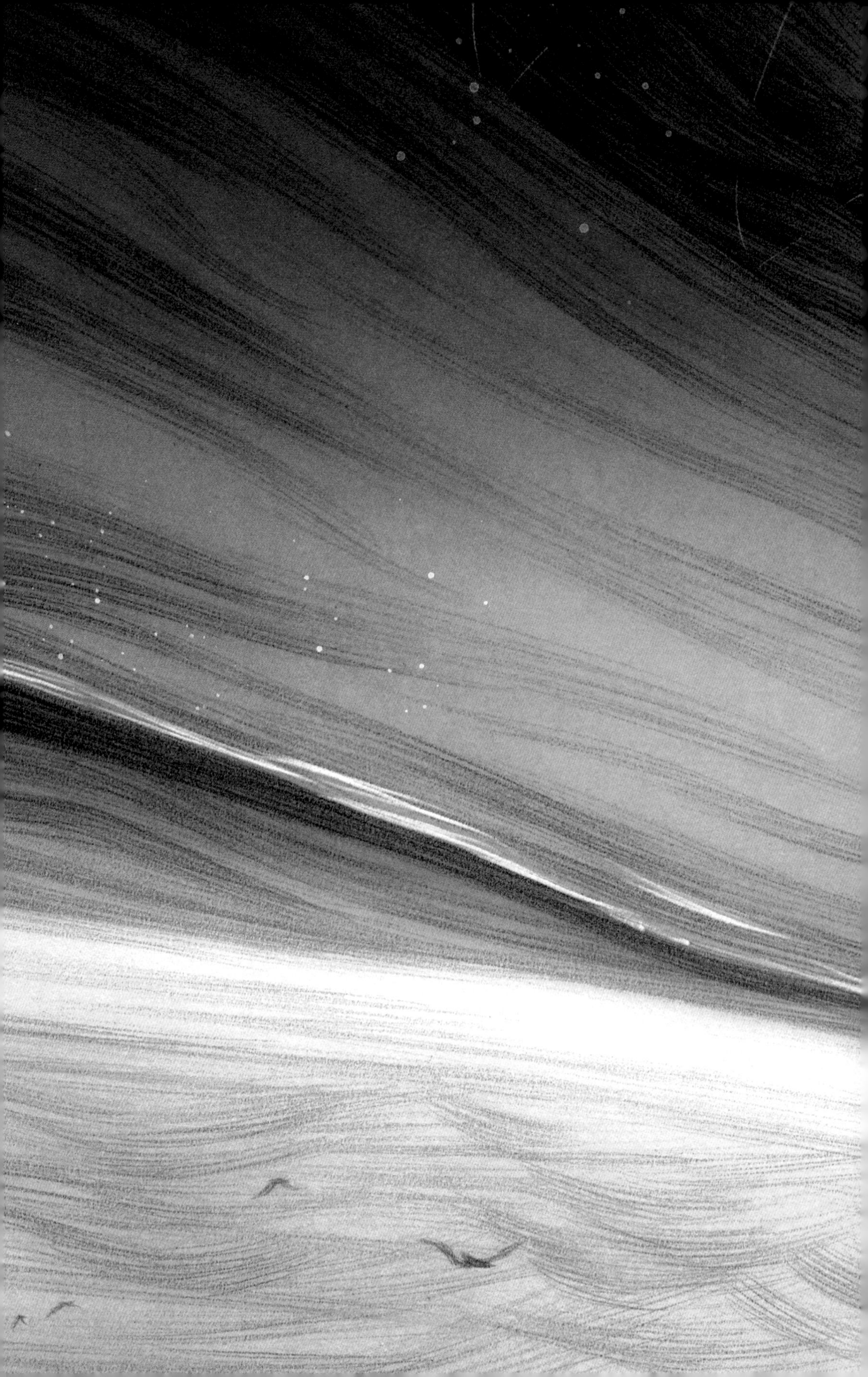

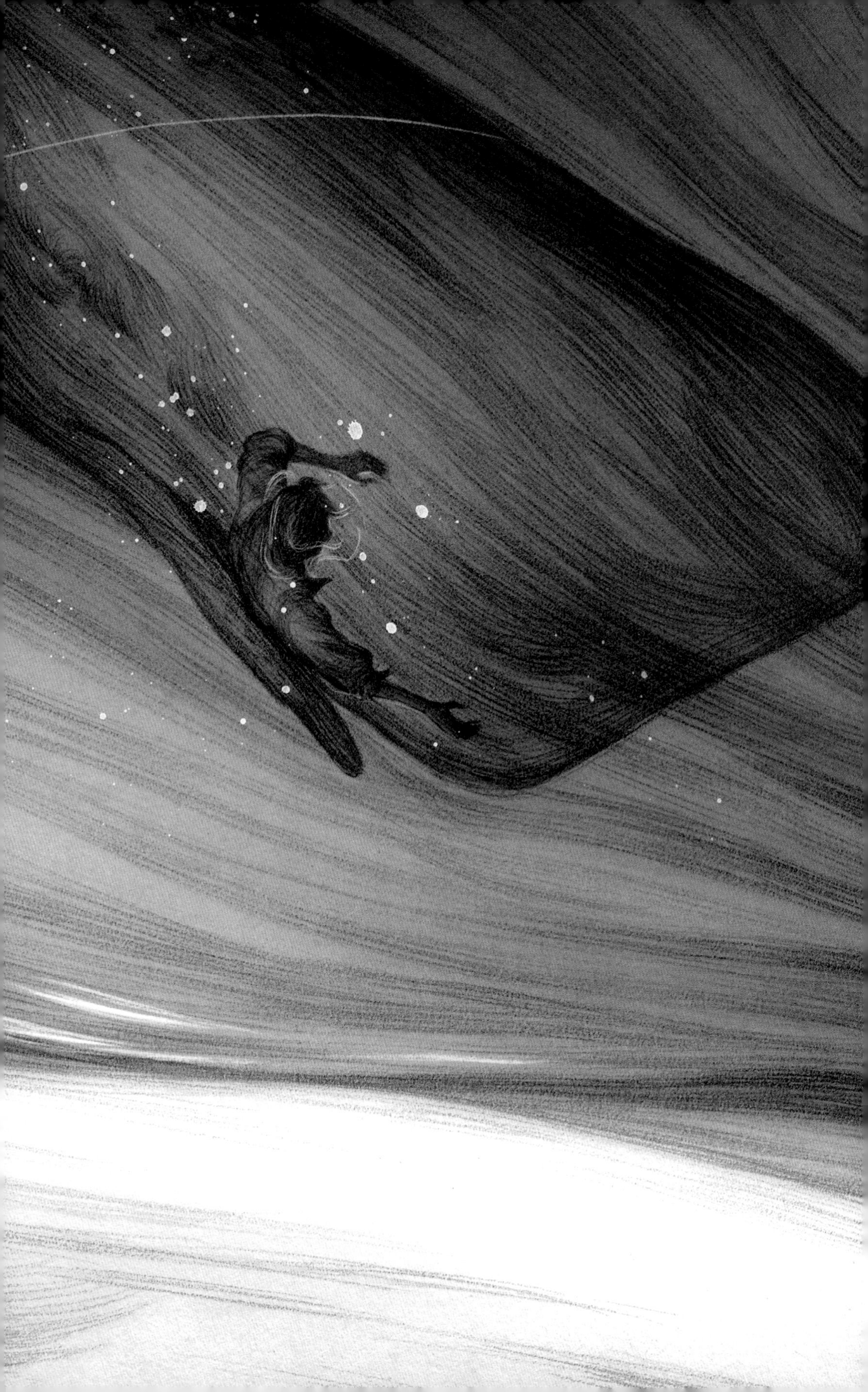

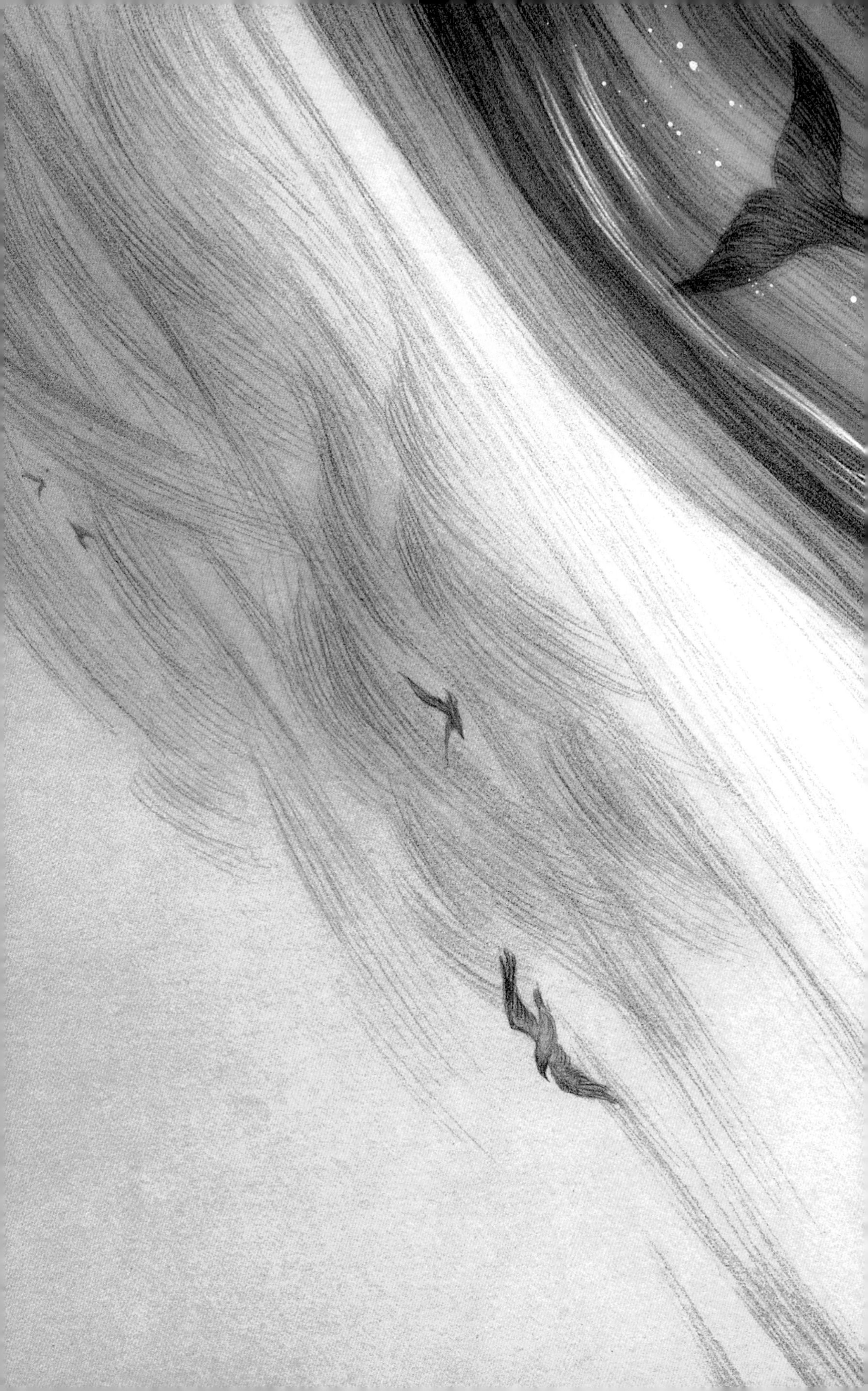

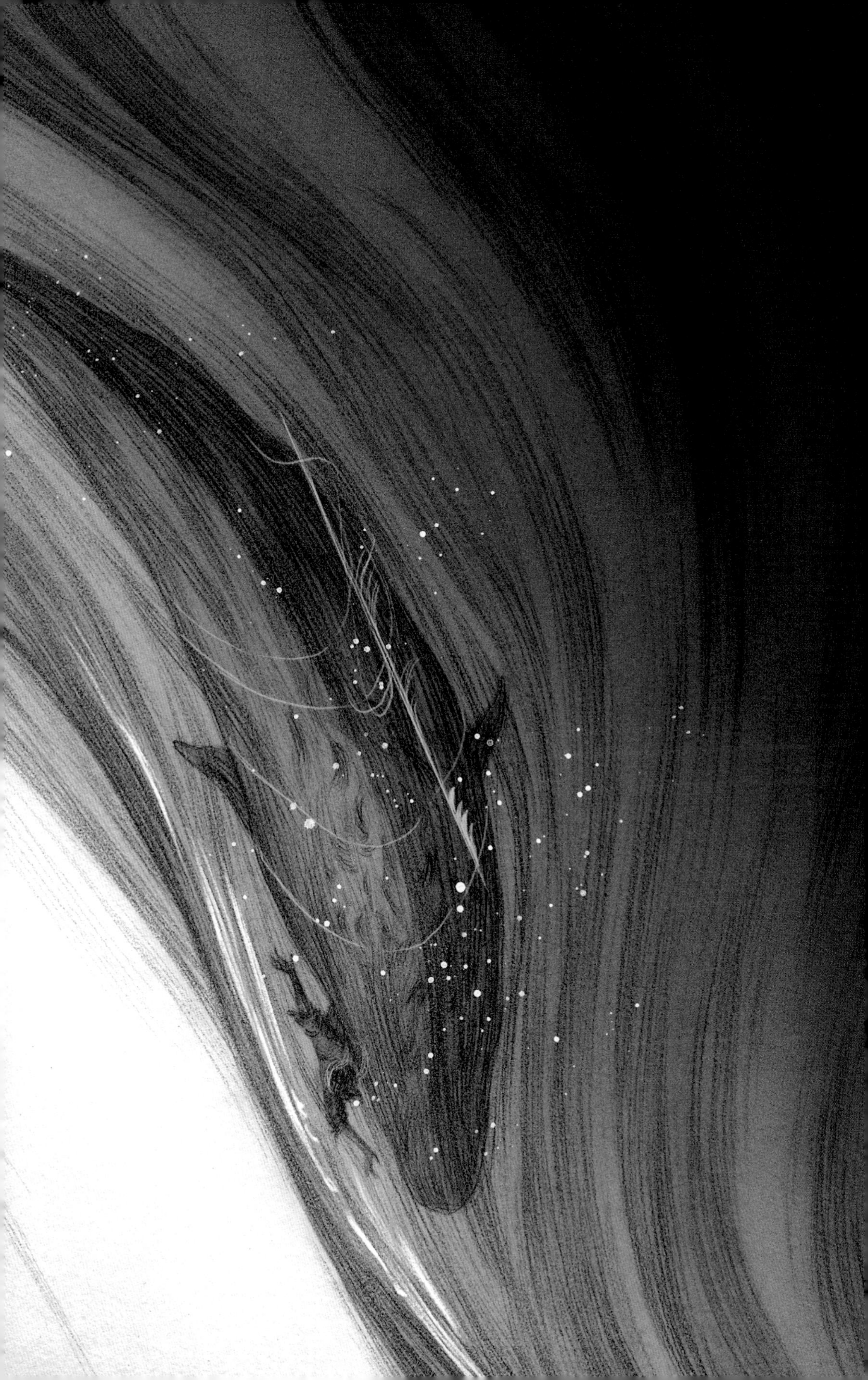

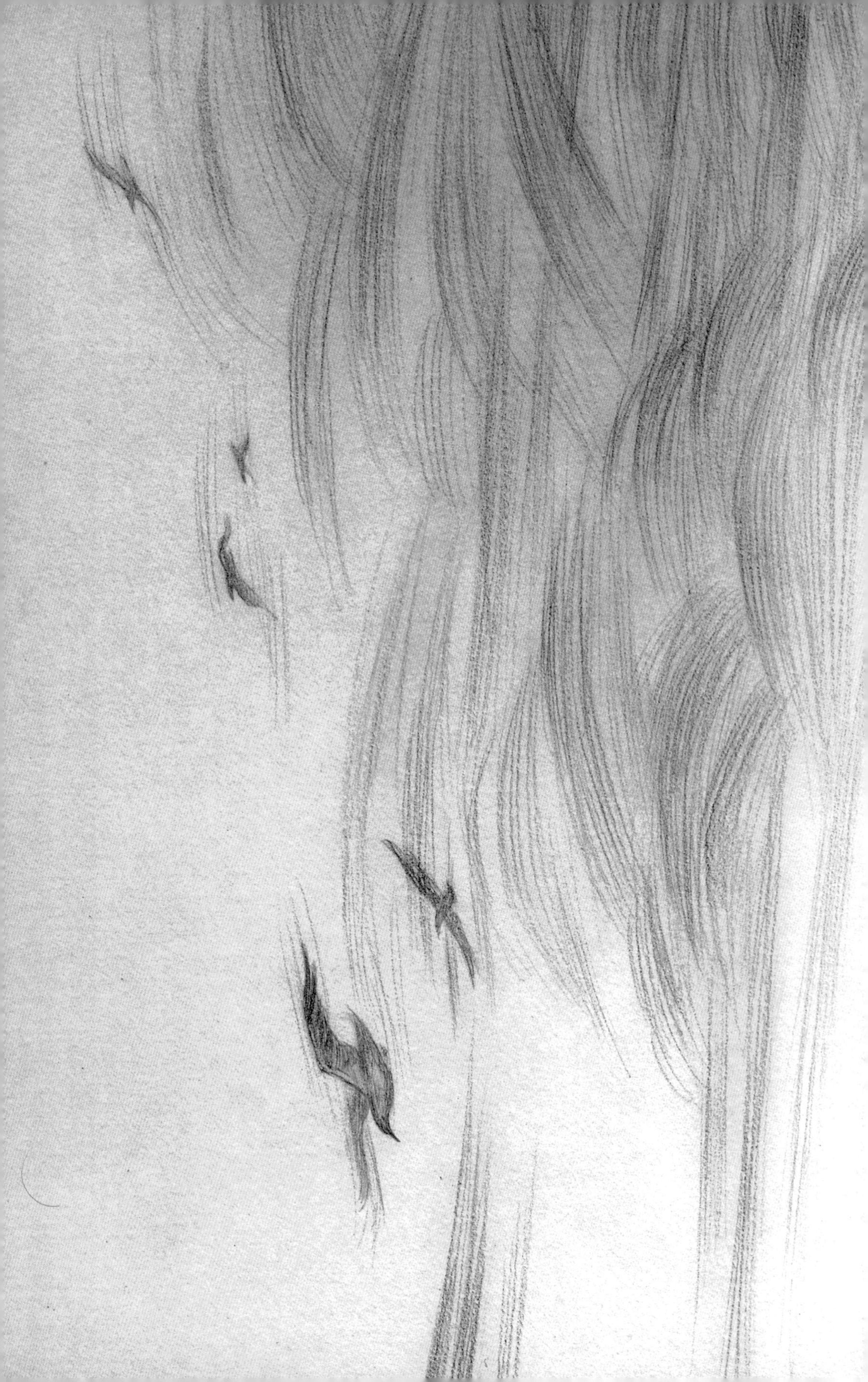

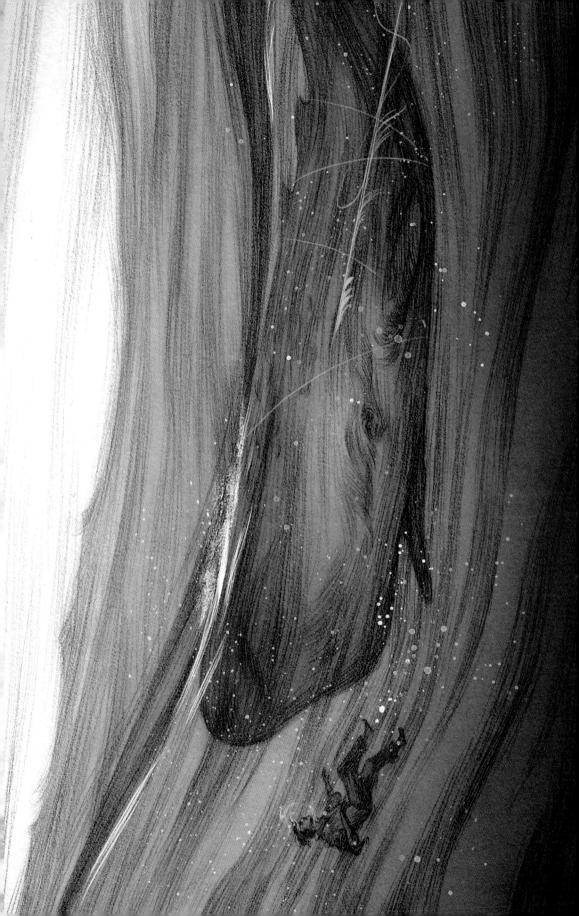

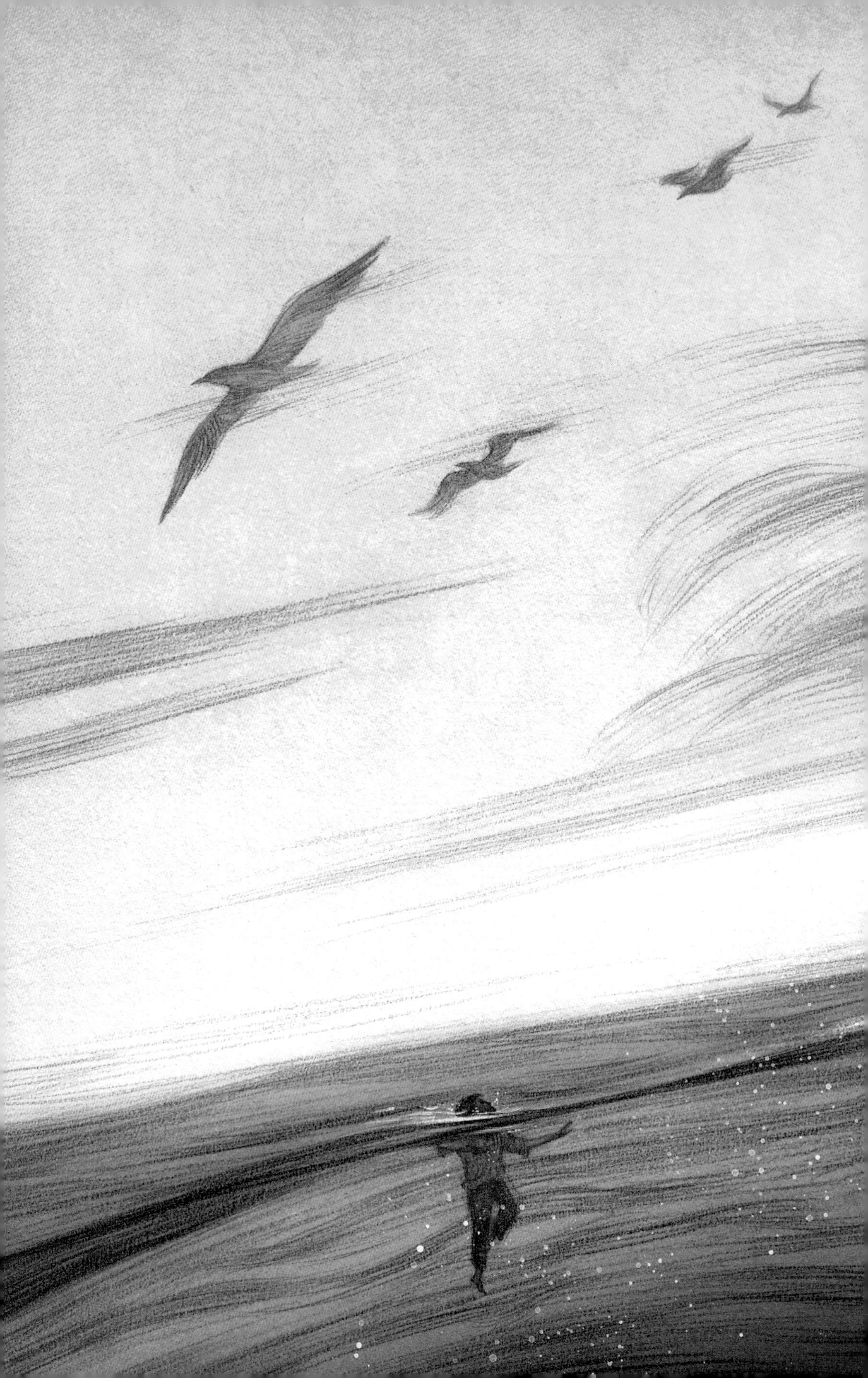

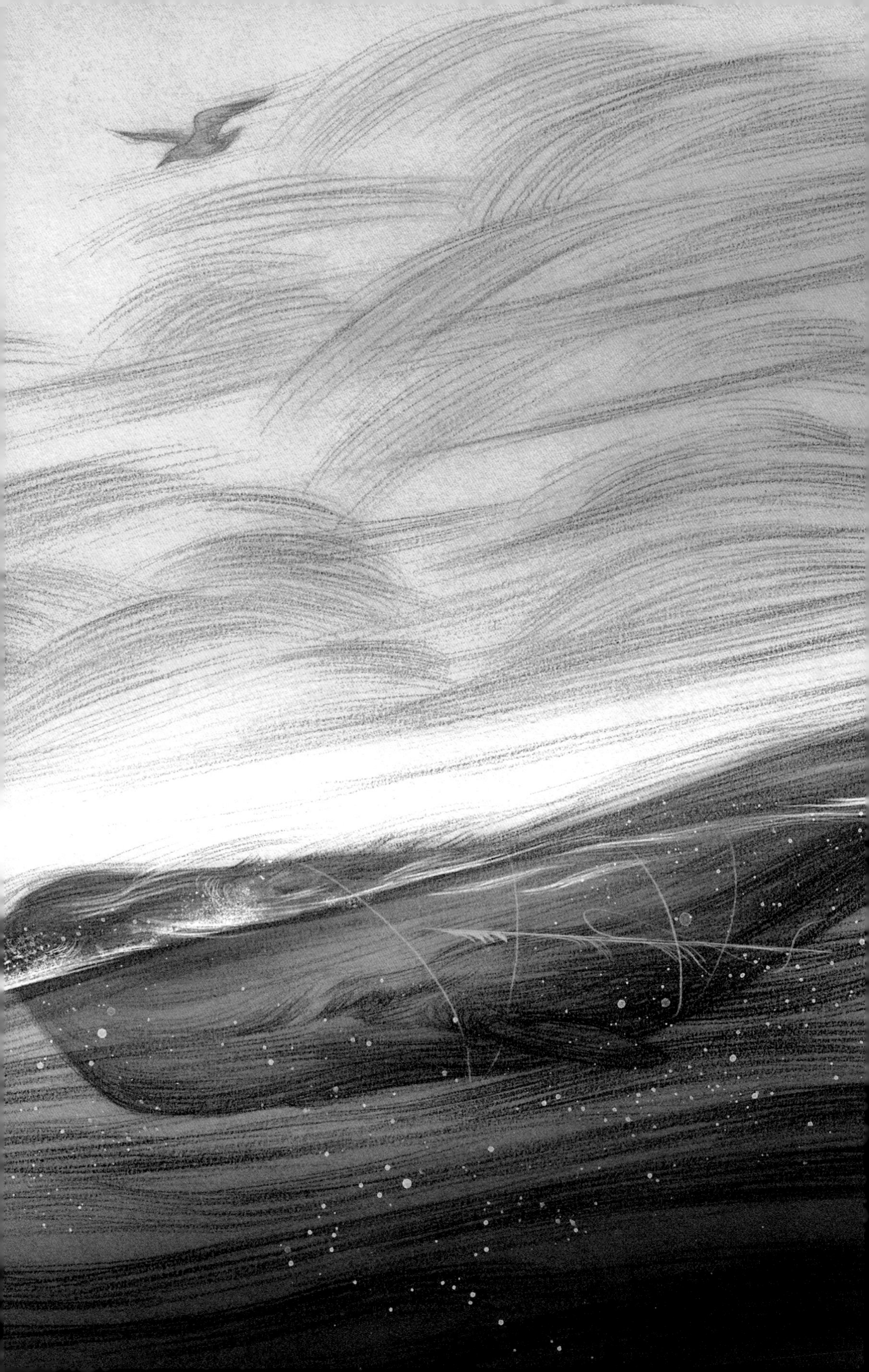

10

I LET HIM GO INTO HIS PRECIOUS AIR. He only coughed more and thrashed at the water. I stayed there with him, unsure what to do after following my Captain's command.

At the very least, I could breathe deeply.

Ah, the Abyss. The dizzying moment when your weight shifts, and the world tilts, up becoming down, the world pulling at your stomach like a gyroscope, and suddenly, there is air to breathe.

We are proud, proud creatures of the ocean. We dominate it, conquer it, there is no creature in it that doesn't flee before us or do our bidding. It is the supreme element, three full dimensions in which to live and race and hunt. We have illuminated its darknesses, husbanded its fish. We have made great cities, grown out from the mountaintops that drop from our sky.

We are the ocean.

And yet, still, the Abyss holds our life. We must breathe. We must. Even with the breather bubbles, we must, all of us, return to the Abyss now and again.

This is our weakness.

The young male struggled his way to a bit of wreckage. He clung on, gasping at the air, while I breathed directly and considered the riddle we had discovered.

The ship was still afloat, but there were dead men in the water. No other pods were in evidence who might have done that, and they certainly would have harvested the bodies before scuttling the ship. And here was the young male, hand stuck into the water, with a message meant for . . . who, exactly? Any hunting pod who happened by?

Or one in particular?

Captain Alexandra, as I said, was famous and infamous. She was known as the hardest-driving, most risk-taking Captain to sail from our ports. This reputation was well-earned. She was a veteran of a thousand hunts. Her Apprentices – the ones who did not die on the Abyss – rose to the highest ranks of their own hunting pods.

I had fought tooth and tail to be chosen as even her humblest Apprentice. If I was going to hunt, I was going to hunt with the best. But that's the risk, isn't it? Being the best gives you nowhere to go but down. It also makes you a target, for if someone else wants to be the best, they have to beat you, don't they?

And perhaps, in the Captain's mind, that included the best hunter men had to offer.

"Bathsheba!" the Captain called from what was now below me. "Has he recovered?"

"He recovers from his drowning," I answered. "I don't know if he will ever recover from his fright."

"Not my concern. Give him another bubble and bring him back. We will have words, the man and I."

She swam back to our ship, now almost fully stocked from the salvage. Even the remnants of their hull were being reclaimed by our sailors, where its wood would be used for repairs. Waste nothing at sea, for it is sometimes a desert and you never know where replenishment may come.

I circled the young male. He still, remarkably, held the disc in his hand, as if he'd forgotten it in his shock. He watched me, his eyes wide. I opened my mouth to bring him back—

"No, please!" he shouted.

I was so surprised to be addressed directly I paused. Men rarely bothered to speak to us. They *never* spoke to Apprentices.

"You're going to kill me," he gasped.

"Yes," I said, struggling with the words, "but not yet. Be calm."

"I didn't ask for this. I am a prisoner."

"I am not interested—"

"I'm not a hunter. I never *wanted* to be a hunter."

My voice hardened. "*Every* man wants to be a hunter."

I took him under, ignoring his pleas. ◆

II

A SURPRISE. I UNDERSTOOD THE YOUNG male best when he spoke.

"Again," the Captain said, losing her patience.

"He is uncatchable," the young male said, only just keeping to this side of hysteria. "That's the message I was to give to you, along with the coin."

The Captain circled once more, trying to decipher his words. "Again," she said.

The young male looked at me in a panic. I made to answer, but Treasure beat me to it. "Toby Wick says you're uncatchable," she said.

"That is not—" I started to say.

"*I'm* uncatchable?" our Captain said, sounding pleased.

"Forgive me, Captain," I said, giving side-eye to Treasure. "The young male says that Toby Wick allegedly calls *himself* uncatchable." The Captain looked considerably less pleased with this. "I believe it's by way of a taunt."

"She's wrong," Treasure said. "Toby Wick knows you're the best Captain in the sea. It's a token of respect."

"Toby Wick isn't *real*," I snapped. "We are being goaded into a chase."

"Of course we are," the Captain said. "But that doesn't

47

mean we can't explore other meanings."

"What are you saying to each other?" the young man said, for we were speaking our own language.

"We are discussing your words," I said to him, without thinking. "What they mean."

I turned to see the Captain and other Apprentices regarding me. The Captain suspiciously, Treasure jealously, Willem fearfully. "Your facility with languages impresses, Bathsheba," our Captain said.

"My grandmother was a teacher," I said, for this was true.

"So she was. You will be our interpreter."

"Captain—"

"Watch that you make no more mistakes though," she said, swimming under the ropes that towed the ship. "I heard what the man said. *I* am uncatchable." She looked to me, warning in her eye. "That was the message, wasn't it, Bathsheba?"

What choice did I have? I was an Apprentice. How was I to know this was the first step that would lead everyone here to their deaths?

"That's right, Captain," I said. "My mistake."

"As I thought. Now, find out where we can start the hunt." ◆

12

THE YOUNG MALE TOLD ME THEY HAD come across none other than Toby Wick and his famous white ship while on their own hunt. Or rather, that is what he gathered, for he saw none of it himself, as he was a prisoner below, for some crime of his own he was vague on. Toby Wick wished to leave a message in the ocean, and he demanded the young male's ship do it for him.

But something went amiss, something between Toby Wick and the ship's Captain.

"I heard them screaming," the young male said. "I heard them dying. Until the Captain himself came down to the brig, made a hole and stuck my hand through. He told me the message I was to give if I survived, but said no more. Then he went above decks and that was the last I heard of him."

"What happened to him?" I asked. "What happened to the crew?"

"I told you, I don't know." He held my gaze, terrified. "But everyone knows Toby Wick is a killer."

"Toby Wick is a myth," I said. "You were boarded by a hostile pod, that's all. Now, tell me about the coin."

For we had finally prised it from his hand and stored it belowdecks.

"It's a map," he told me. "The triangles are mountains."

"There are many mountains in the ocean," I said.

"Please," he said. "I'm cold."

I stopped, surprised. I considered that he almost certainly *was* cold. For a man. We had swam up into the depths, far from the surface of the Abyss; I kept needing to enlarge his breather bubble as the pressure made it shrink. Plus, we were moving quickly now, the currents pushing past his body, taking away all its precious heat.

I swam to the Captain, to where she pulled the ship from the front. "He will die if we do not warm him," I said.

"His life matters not to me. It is the information I want."

"If he dies, the information dies with him. He has no blubber. He will perish quite soon."

The Captain sighed. "One heater crab from the hold."

"Two would be better—"

For that, a strike across my head from her tail, enough to jar my teeth together.

"One," the Captain repeated, needlessly.

I swam, head throbbing, back to the ship, ordering a

sailor to bring me a single heater crab. I took it over to the young male, spitting it at his chest. He screamed as it landed on him, but we had bound him to our mast so he couldn't get away. He didn't *stop* screaming until he realized the chemical reaction from the crab's underside was generating a small warmth.

He gasped inside his breather bubble, shrinking it again. I was forced to fill it once more from my own supply. "You must breathe less heavily," I said. "Or you will drown."

"I am upside down but feel right side up. It is very strange."

"It is the way of this world," I said. "We feel it when we breach."

"I have lost my mind," he said. "This can only be a nightmare."

"It may be, but you have it in your own power to end it."

"You mean tell you everything and then die."

"Yes, that is what I mean. But there are many ways to die. Fast and slow."

"If a man and a whale speak," he said, as if it were a well-known saying, "one must perish."

"Not always. There have been peace talks."

"Failures. All of them."

"You hunt us."

"You hunt *us*."

"And so it has always been, and so it always shall be. Now, speak more of your message, and do so quickly."

The young male seemed, almost all of a sudden, to accept his fate. He breathed a few more times, then he said, "You are to head east-south-east."

"And who told you this?" I sneered. "Toby Wick himself?"

"Of course not."

"For Toby Wick is a *bedtime story—*"

"*Someone* attacked the ship while I was chained in the hold. *Someone* bloodied my Captain before he drilled a hole in his own hull."

"Tell me about the mountains. For *my* Captain wishes to know."

"You are to wait offshore of the third."

"Offshore?" I said. "These mountains reach into the Abyss?"

"The what?"

"Your world. The air below."

"The air above," he corrected.

"It's all a matter of point of view, is it not?"

"That's what you call where we live? The Abyss?"

"Yes. Is this not known?"

"No, it's just . . ." He looked around at the ocean passing by, the great deep blues, the cold black heights, lit up here and there by distant floating cities, the stars in our sky. "That's what we call this."

"Do you?" I said, genuinely startled. "But there is so much life here."

"Bathsheba!" called the Captain. "Answers!"

I immediately left the young male to tell her what I had learned, but as I went, he said an odd word after me, one I didn't understand. "What?" I said, turning back.

"Demetrius," he said. "It is my name."

I looked at him for a moment longer, this enemy of mine, this prey, this threat to our lives so persistent that our entire culture developed around it, as theirs had around us. This creature I would kill without a thought, or if I did, the thought would be of a reckoning, a balance made of competing currents. This frightened, pathetically small *man*. A prisoner, first of men, now of us, not even proper *crew*.

Who said he never wanted to hunt.

I surprised myself by saying "Bathsheba" before I swam away. ◆

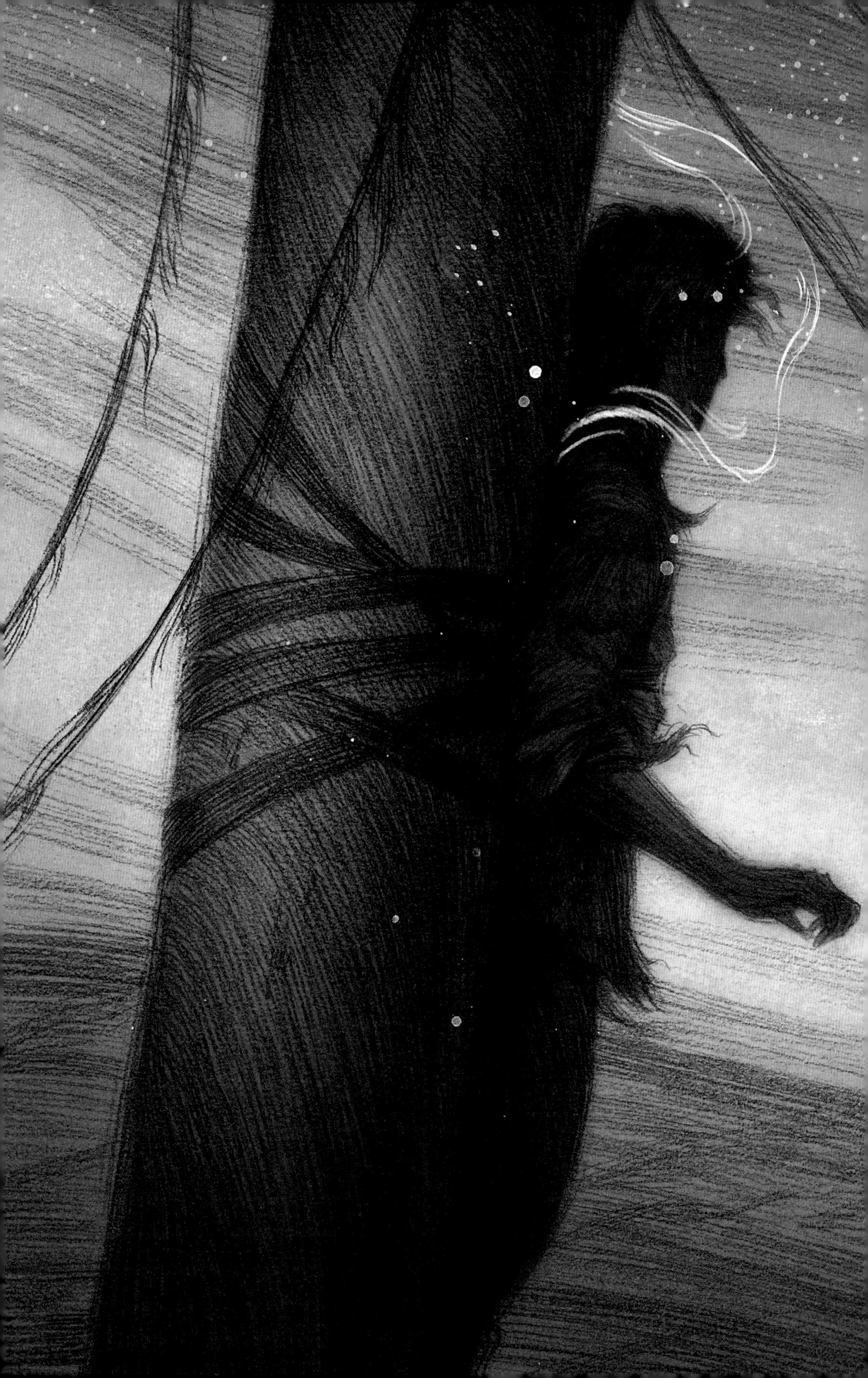

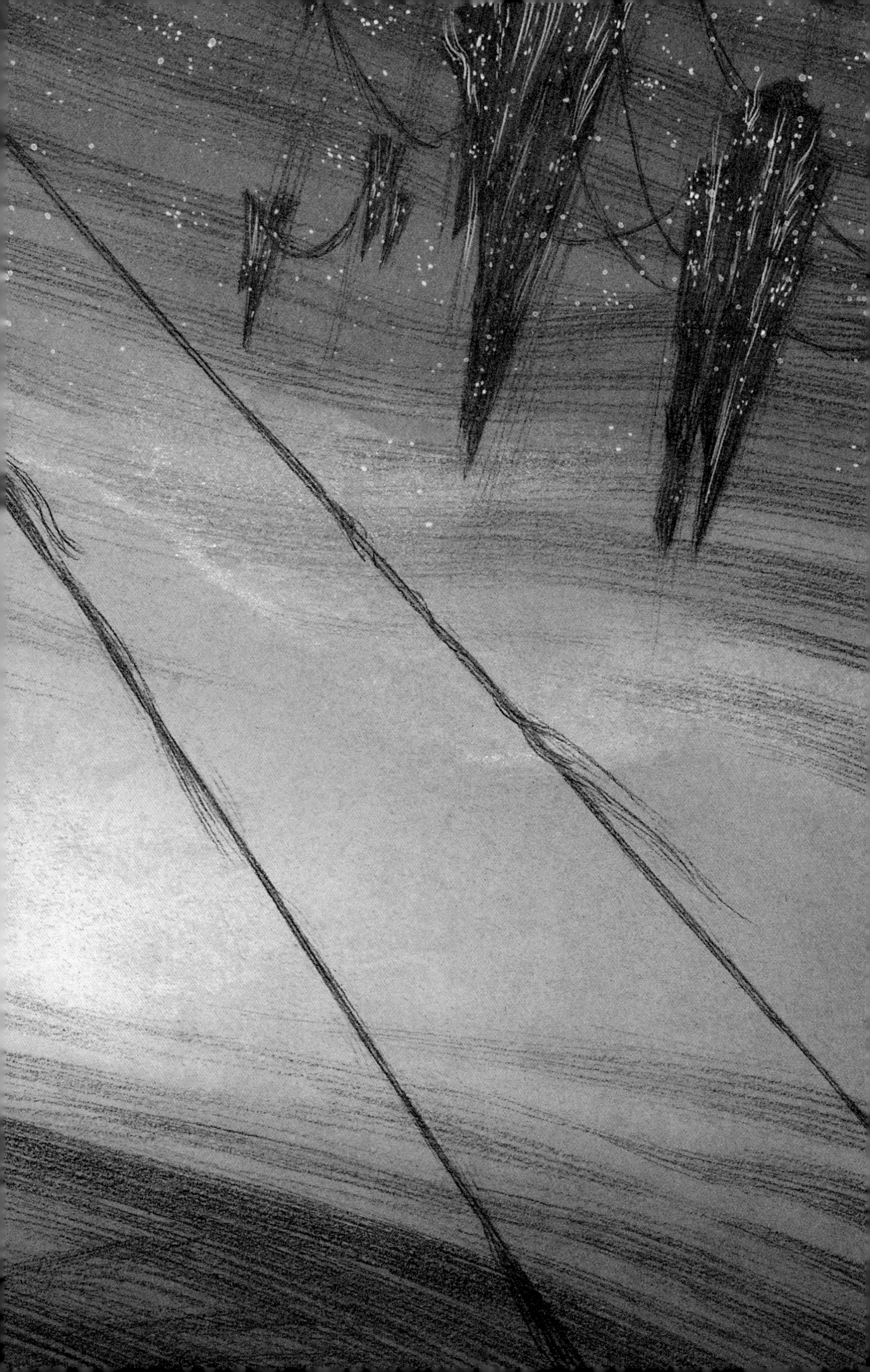

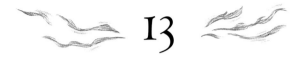

13

HERE IS WHY I DID NOT BELIEVE. WHY I *knew* the myth of Toby Wick to be only that. I will tell you once. It's all my heart can stand.

The second year of training before you leave on your first hunt is shipbuilding, for who knows when an Apprentice might be called upon to aid a sinking whale-ship? The ship-building bays — swathes of open water near common men-ship graveyards, from which we reap most of our material — were distant from my home city, and to travel between, we moved in large pods. Men patrolled their side of the Abyss and we ours, but no one's safety was guaranteed.

My mother was coming to visit, to see how I was doing. I knew she worried. Her messages only barely concealed it, though even the small attempt at concealment made me miss her.

I had made a small storage-ship (as all trainees did), smaller even than myself, having found every last board on my own in the men-ship graveyard, swimming among the great masted ships men so frequently lost in storms in that part of the sea, their lack of mastery of traveling in weather not even the least useless thing about them. I was proud of my wee storage-ship, eager for my mother to see my progress, maybe even calm her worries some about this destiny I seemed to be following.

She left with a traveling pod, and I waited for her to arrive. And I waited. And I waited. Until finally, the shipyard master — my teacher — swam urgently to me from the open ocean.

"Blood in the water," he said. Only those words, and I was already swimming as fast as my tail could push. "It's too late!" he called after me. But he followed, for which I will always honor him.

We were the first to the slaughter.

The pod my mother traveled with was mostly gone, the sloppy harvesting of men already begun. My mother was one of the few who still fled. I saw her first in my echolocation. Then I saw the launches of men pursuing her with a vengeance that seemed unhinged, even for them.

My mother, though sometimes unfocused to a degree that maddened me, sometimes dreamy enough for me to blame her as the reason my father never returned from the farms he helped run, was a remarkable athlete when she put her mind to it. She could beat them. She would.

"Mother!" I called and tried to swim faster, putting myself at terrible risk. My echolocation refined and I could see the harpoons already in her body, attached to barrels that made it harder for her to escape to the depths of the ocean above. But she was ahead of them now, gaining in distance.

"Bathsheba!" I heard her yell. "Get away!"

It was only when she swam into my actual vision that I saw why. A second ship, a full sailing vessel, not another launch, cut brutally across the Abyss from a direction I hadn't even bothered clicking in.

"Turn back!" was the last thing my mother said before the men were on her. It was only the shipyard master's much greater size that prevented me from swimming to her anyway and meeting the same fate. Instead, I could only watch as they murdered her, sloppily, wastefully, prolonging her suffering until finally casting her to the sharks as so much trash.

I am not alone in my hurt. I would never pretend to be so. Every whale has been affected, directly or not, by the actions of men. I took my broken heart (still beating, I can feel it even now) and hid it away inside myself, deep and geologic, like a volcanic vent, unseen but making the ocean around it boil.

They would pay. There would never be enough of them to pay fully.

And now, here, I tell you why I say "they."

The myth of Toby Wick, of his great white hull, was it him? Was he the Captain of the ship that killed her? The hull was white, though that could have been barnacles.

But no, my eyes saw her die, and my eyes saw no devil. They only saw the men who did it.

Men. Not myths. Certainly not the myths that followed this attack. Even the shipyard master started speaking of how it must have been Toby Wick himself who took on and slaughtered a pod that size, how no fierce group of whales could be taken by anything less than a devil.

But I saw what I saw.

Here is the truth behind the myth: all men are Toby Wick.

For who needs devils when you have men? ◆

14

WE SWAM EAST-SOUTH-EAST AT A PUNISHING pace, the Captain's great bulk towing our ship, we Apprentices in drafting position behind her. Our job on the trek was to keep the ship in her slipstream while the sailors adjusted our sails to catch the currents, lightening her load.

It was not thrilling work.

"Don't men lie?" Willem said, glancing over to the mast where our young man – Demetrius, as I had not yet decided to think of him – was still tied.

"Always," Treasure said. "It is the basis of their culture. They can never be trusted. Never."

"Then why does the Captain follow what the man says?" I asked, out of nothing more than annoyance at her certainty.

"She is wily," Treasure said. "She knows she is being lied to. She is merely preparing."

"How?" Willem asked, in seeming innocence. Though perhaps only seeming. You did not get to be Second Apprentice on the *Alexandra* by being daft.

"That's for the Captain to know," Treasure snapped, and if my story makes her seem unpleasant and paranoid and a suck-up, that's because she was unpleasant and paranoid and a suck-up. "Know your place, Second Apprentice."

Willem looked over to me with a wink.

"Just think," Treasure said, her own eyes glazing with foreseen glory, "we will be the ones who take Toby Wick once and for all. We will be part of the legend of our Captain. We will be legends ourselves."

"Or maybe the disc is symbolic," Willem said, half dreamily. "Maybe they're not mountains at all. There are three peaks. There are three Apprentices. The disc is a precious metal, what men use for tender. Perhaps the three marks mean that the price Toby Wick will extract is the Captain's three Apprentices."

"You're wrong," Treasure said to Willem. "The disc is a prophecy."

I groaned internally at this word. "Not everything is a prophecy."

Treasure rounded on me. "A hand sticking through the hull of a man ship, meant for *us*—"

"We don't know that—"

"Sending us to three mountains, where we shall all meet our destiny. Perhaps Willem is partially right. The three marks *are* the three Apprentices. The disc is our Captain. But Toby Wick has given himself over to our oblivion. It is prophecy of the purest sort."

We are always saying things like this, us as a people. *Prophecy of the purest sort.* What does that even mean? If prophecy were pure, it would be fact, but it is not. And yet how it drives us, even when all I have ever seen is that the only prophecy that has any accuracy — any *purity* — is the one that self-fulfils.

We would get to the mountains. We would meet our destiny. But was it a disc that made it true? Or our dogged pursuit of it? Will the world end in darkness because it is foretold? Or because there will be those who believe it so strongly they will make it so? In the fear that I always try to hide in my heart, I wonder if there is even a difference. ◆

15

THE NEXT DAY, TREASURE SUDDENLY ROSE from her duties, scanning the empty ocean. I could hear the clicks of her echolocation. She swam hurriedly to the Captain, who listened closely to her. Then both turned to us.

"Parley," the Captain said. "A pod approaches."

Our sailors instantly switched the sails to drag, slowing the ship so that the Captain could release herself from the tow ropes. The rest of us were already at work, helping to turn the ship to best defensive advantage.

"Not you, Bathsheba," the Captain said. "You will hide our captive." Her great forehead loomed over me threateningly. "No one shall hear of Toby Wick's prophecy except those for whom it is meant."

So the prophecy had already become something so valuable it must be kept secret.

"Aye, Captain," I said. "But we are in clear ocean. Won't that mean—"

"You will have to take him in the hull."

I blew some bubbles out of my blowhole in alarm. "But Captain—"

Without warning, she opened her mouth and bit my forehead, the single most humiliating thing one of our kind can do to another. My chest burned with the outrage, though I could do nothing but submit. Out of the corner of my eye, I saw Willem and Treasure watching with a terrified glee.

"You came to me with vengeance in your eye, Third Apprentice," she said, in almost a growl. "You came to me promising death and blood in the water. But instead of letting me deliver that to you, you have somehow entered into the belief that my commands are not commands, but openings for discussion. This is the second time. There will not be a third."

"Aye, Captain," I said, pained.

"You will go into the hold with our captive. You will keep him there and alive. Or you will no longer be Third Apprentice."

She let me go, small streams of blood flowing from my head, top and bottom, where her teeth cut it. The school of blue sharks that always followed us at a wary distance visibly perked up, though they could only still be gorged on the leftover men from yesterday.

I swam, humiliated, to the young male. "What's happening?" he asked. I didn't answer, just took him in my jaws — too roughly; he cried out, sputtering more water — tearing him loose from the mast and swimming to the stern of our ship.

Where I took him inside. ◆

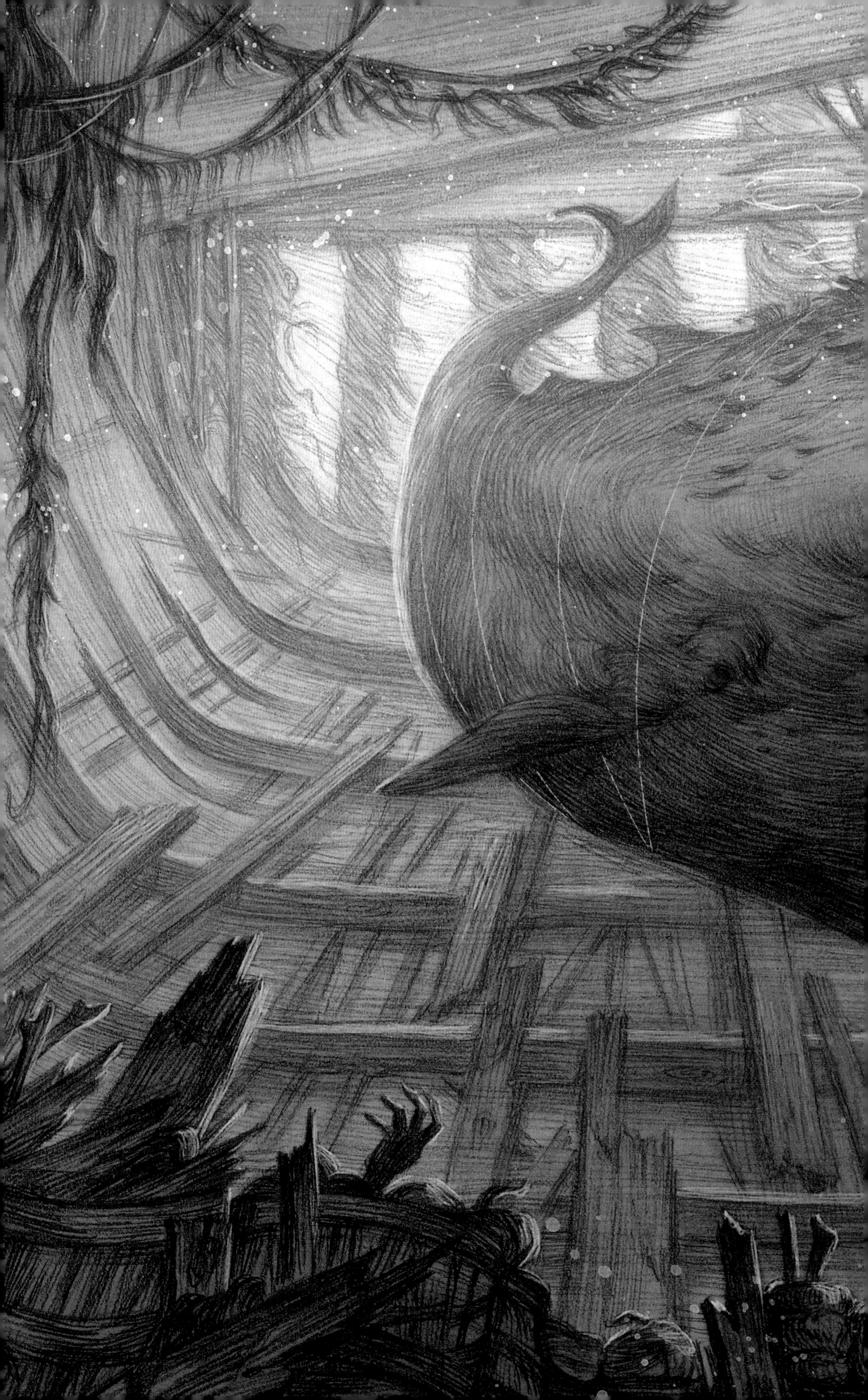

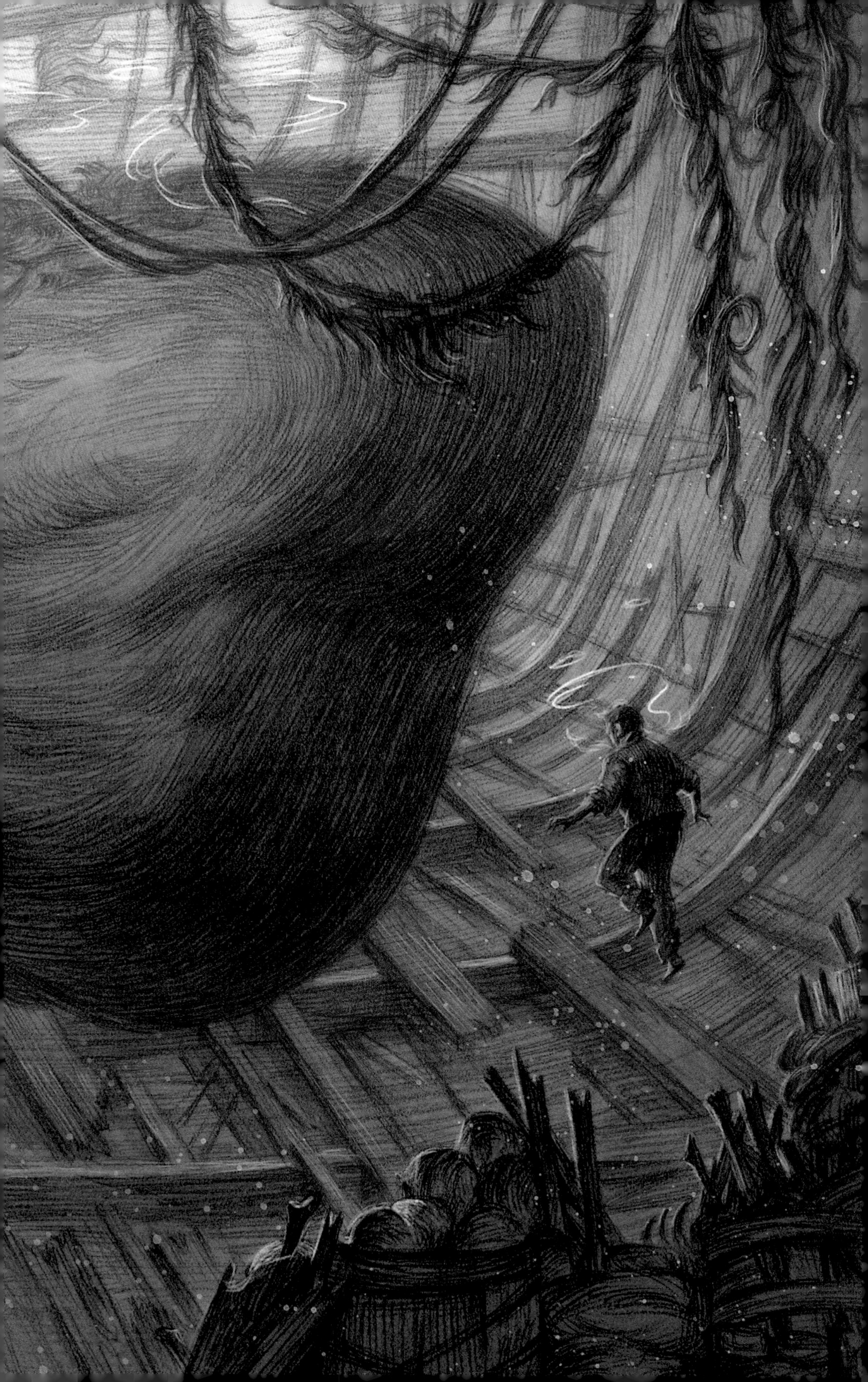

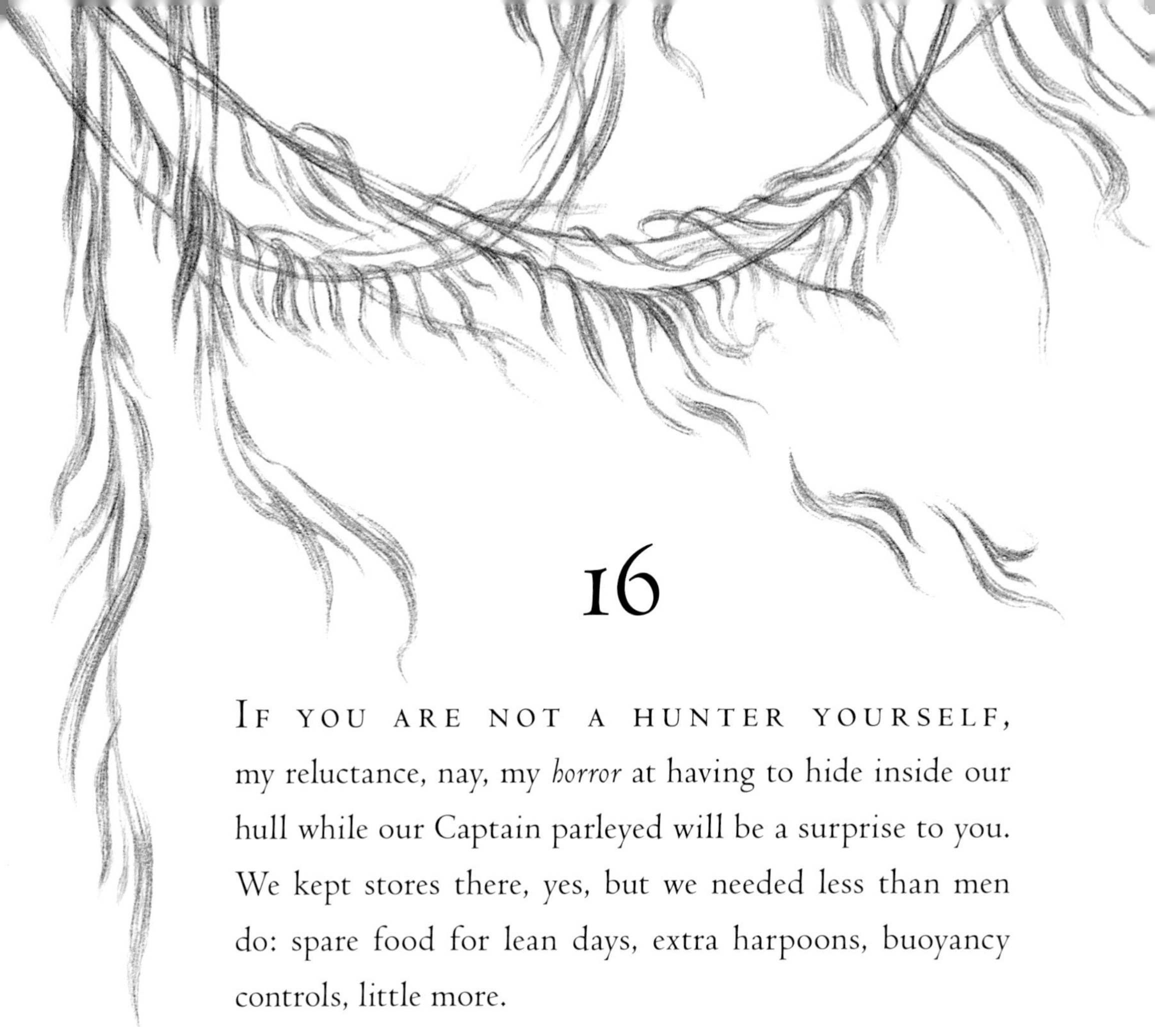

16

If you are not a hunter yourself, my reluctance, nay, my *horror* at having to hide inside our hull while our Captain parleyed will be a surprise to you. We kept stores there, yes, but we needed less than men do: spare food for lean days, extra harpoons, buoyancy controls, little more.

It was mainly a slaughterhouse. A rendering plant, where we kept the bodies and spoils of all we hunted. A place of ghosts, crying out in their nonsense language. A dead and stinking place.

A place which it was the worst luck in the sea to enter without a kill.

I swam the young male – Demetrius, I suppose – into the empty hull, an obedient sailor closing it behind me, plunging us into a darkness lifted only by small square windows that looked out into the ocean.

"What is this place?" he asked. "Are you going to kill me?"

"I will if you do not keep quiet," I said, eyeing our surroundings, despite a strong wish not to.

I knew the instant Demetrius did the same. Even with his man eyes, unsuitable for the gloom of the ocean, he could still see the limbs of his former shipmates tied in bunches, their torsos bundled into bales, their heads bumping one another in great coral jugs. The water was murky with blood and flesh, small fish eating the floating bits.

Demetrius was quiet, seeing it all, his mouth agape (how tiny were their mouths, how useless to eat anything but one bite at a time, how oh how did they contend for mastery of the world with us for so long?).

"You are monsters," he whispered.

"My mother's head was severed from her body while she yet lived," I whispered back, ferocious in my quiet. "Her body stripped of its fat, then dumped into the ocean for the sharks to eat. You aren't even *efficient* monsters."

"This is a horror," he said. "A hell."

"One you will join if you do not keep still."

For even now I heard it from inside the cursed hull.

Another pod was coming for a parley. ◆

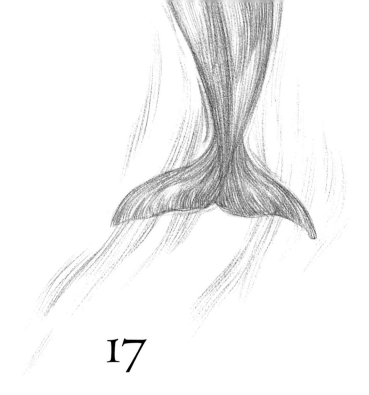

17

"Permission to approach," the other Captain said. This was required for all parleys; if our Captain declined for any other reason than plague on our ship, however, it would be considered an act of aggression. Though aggression was never far away whatever the case.

"Permission granted," our Captain said.

"I am Arcturus," the other Captain said. "We swim from the western ocean."

"And I am Alexandra. We swim from the southern. You are far from home, Captain."

"We have been on the hunt for nearly four years."

This was a remarkable statement. Most hunts lasted a year, two at the very most. Ours was nearing its projected end, though the exact date was always at the whim of the

Captain. Who knew when we would finish, now that we were on the hunt for Toby Wick?

"Are you the pod that took the bounty yesterday?" the other Captain asked, though the weight of our hull and the bones currently boiling on our deck made the question as much a formality as his permission request.

"Aye," our Captain answered. "A weak bounty, but we make do."

"Only two Apprentices? Was one lost?"

"One is on a mission. We are not missing any crew."

"Do you hear that, boys?" Captain Arcturus was, I assumed, talking to his own Apprentices. Crews didn't have to be single gender, but apparently his was as much as ours. "The good Captain sends her Apprentices out on missions. What does this tell you? That she trusts her Apprentices? That she uses them to further her hunt?"

"It tells us that she has more than one mission," one of *Arcturus*'s Apprentices answered.

"It tells us that our hunt is purer," said another.

"It tells us that we outnumber her," said the third.

Our Captain didn't respond to this threat. You never did to that of Apprentices. If you took the insult, you were the weaker one. She rightly left it to her own Apprentices to answer.

"It tells you she has trained her Apprentices to be more than sucker fish," said Treasure, and for a moment, even I was proud of her.

"It tells you she is unafraid of meeting another pod in this wide ocean even with only two Apprentices," said Willem.

"It tells you she is the legendary Captain Alexandra," said Treasure, "and the rules she makes are her own."

"It tells you she is uncatchable," Willem said, and even before she finished, I knew it was going wrong. "Toby Wick himself says so."

An uncomfortable silence in which only the currents could be heard.

"Toby Wick?" Captain Arcturus said, a spike of curiosity in his voice.

"I'm afraid my own legend has grown mythic," said our Captain. "My Apprentices can be overeager in their worship. Obviously, a problem *you* don't have to contend with."

"Our Captain also hunts Toby Wick!" the other ship's First Apprentice said, angrily.

"Silence," Captain Arcturus said, in a voice so calm, I began to wonder for the first time if our Captain had met her match. "We *all* hunt Toby Wick," he continued. "In the sense that the hunt is never over. In the sense that the hunt, *every* hunt, has only a single aim."

"The eradication of man," our Captain said.

"The eradication of man," Captain Arcturus agreed.

"Because who among us would be fool enough to go after the man himself?"

"Who indeed?"

Another quiet, the ocean tending to its own mysterious concerns.

"Well," Captain Arcturus said. "We have no news or messages to offer for the direction you are heading."

This was the traditional wrapping-up. Ships of old would carry news and post from ships they met out in the open ocean. Our cities now were numerous enough to reduce the necessity, but it was still custom to offer.

"Nor do we," our Captain said. "I think we've gathered all the information we need from this parley."

"Indeed," said Captain Arcturus. "Good hunting, Captain. Parley concluded."

"Parley concluded."

I heard the pod begin to move away, with many clicks sent back to us, many more sent to the hull where Demetrius and I were hidden.

"You won't beat him," he whispered to me in the dark.

I thought he was speaking of Arcturus. "He's merely a braggart. Our Captain could defeat him with very little—"

"Toby Wick," he said. "It's what they were talking about, wasn't it? The only words I understood were that name. You won't beat him. He's not a man. He is a devil."

"*If* he exists, he is merely a man."

"A man no other man has ever seen and lived to tell," he said. "A man all of us fear."

I was surprised at this. "No living man has seen him?"

"Nor any whale who has survived. Or so the legends have it."

"Why would Toby Wick kill men?"

"Because he can."

I watched him, warily. "You have let your devil get away from you."

He looked genuinely confused. "To what other purpose is a devil?" ◆

18

"THEY WILL FOLLOW US," CAPTAIN ALEXANDRA said after we were on our way again.

"Let them," Treasure said, defiant.

"You have that much confidence in your Captain?"

"I do." Treasure was almost visibly inflated with pride.

Our Captain turned to Willem and me. "And what of my other Apprentices?"

"I would follow my Captain anywhere," Willem said simply, no doubt truthfully.

"Bathsheba?"

"I hunt men," I said. "And you are the Captain who finds them."

"And Toby Wick? Will I find him, too?"

"All men are Toby Wick, and there is no one better at finding them than you, Captain."

"That almost sounds like prophecy," she said, humor in her voice. She looked at me, as if trying to read my mind. "Perhaps it will be you, our doubter, who puts the harpoon in the side of Toby Wick himself."

"Not if my harpoon is first," Treasure said.

"Or mine," Willem joined in.

Our Captain made a contented sound at their enthusiasm, then spoke some final words to me. "Bathsheba, our captive . . . ?"

"Yes, Captain?"

"There can only be so many answers left," she said. "Find me all of his." She turned deep into the current, pulling our ship. "And then kill him." ◆

73

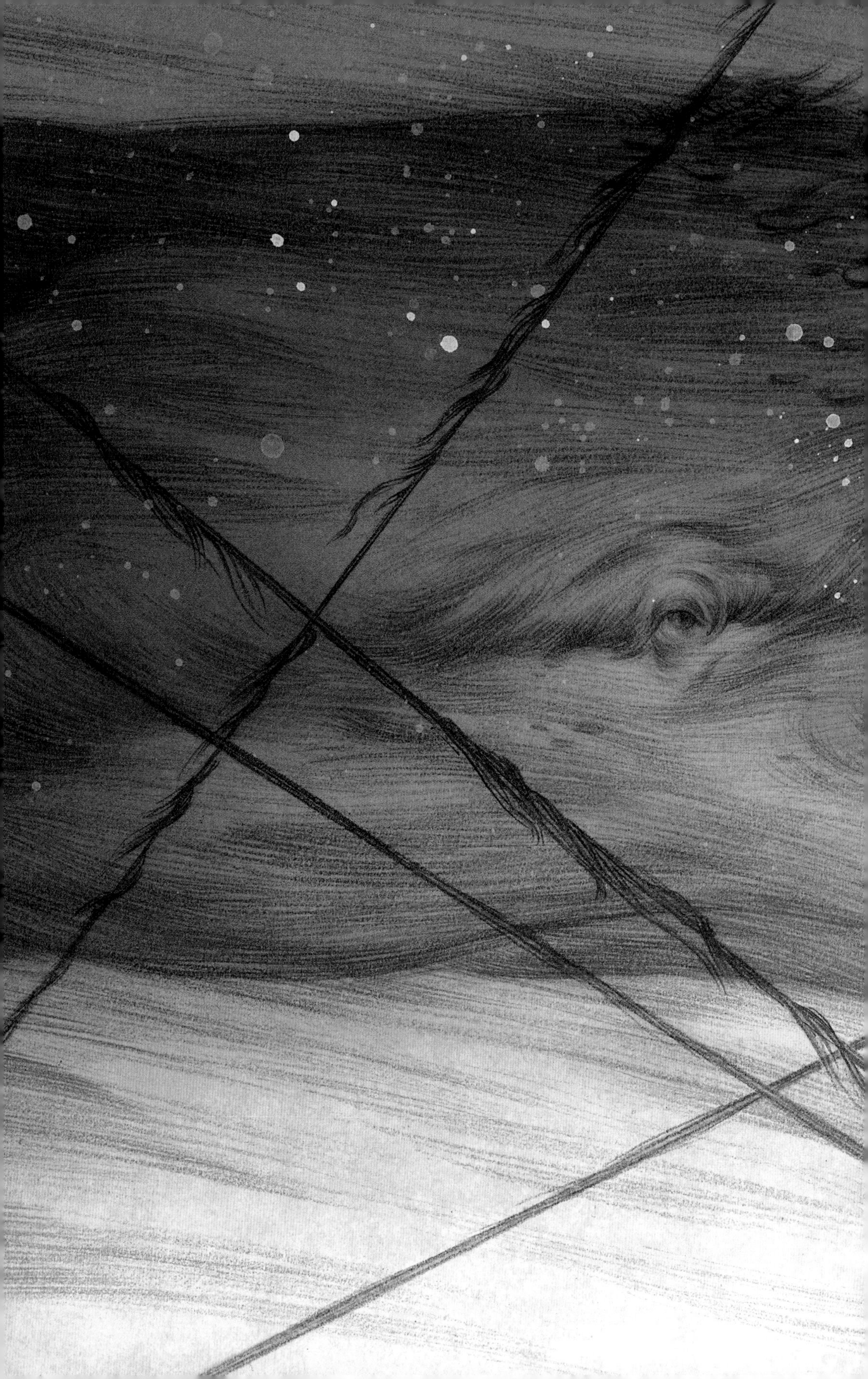

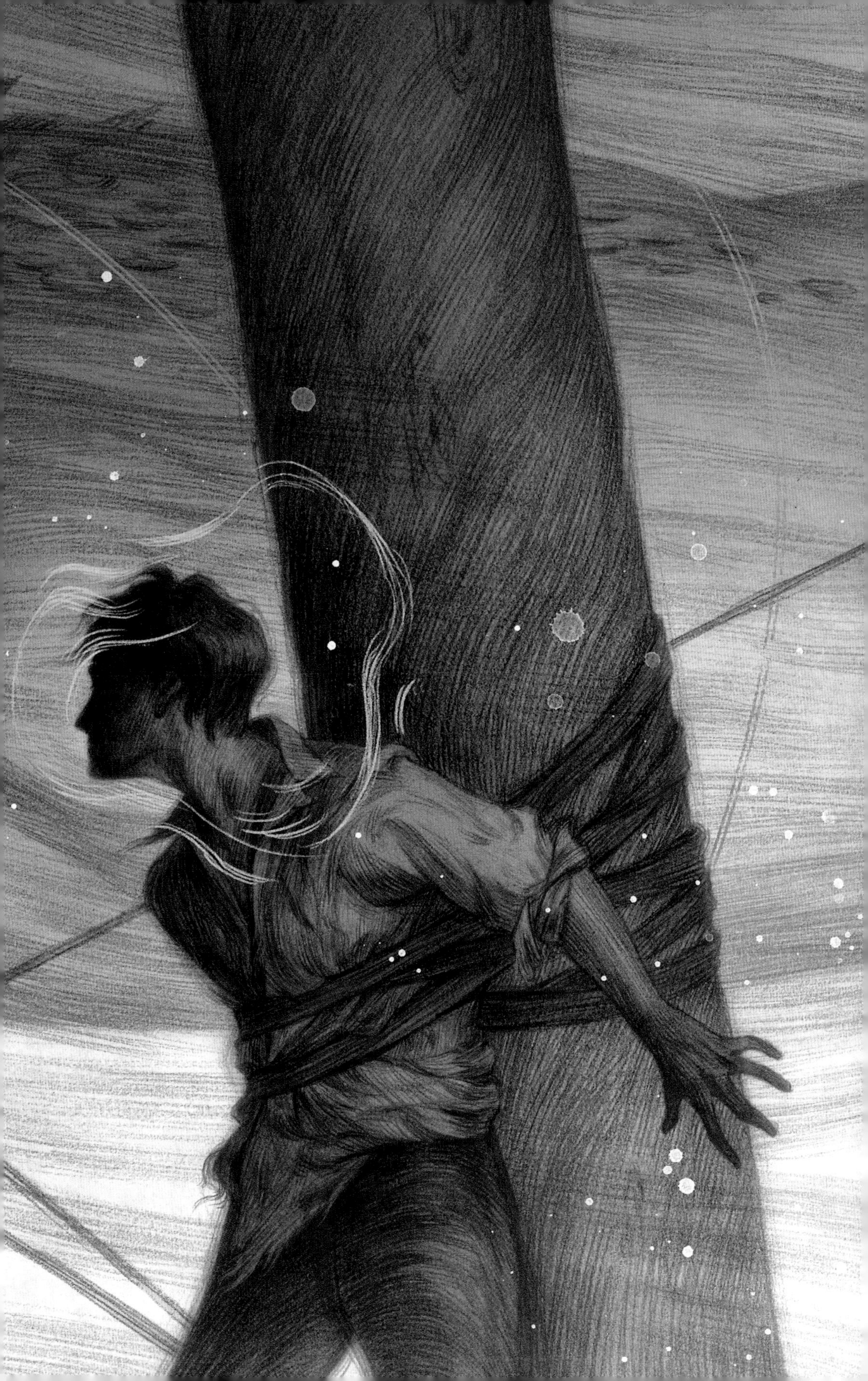

19

I SWAM BACK TO THE MAST WHERE DEMETRIUS
had been retied by the sailors. His head lolled in the current,
the breather bubble lolling with him. I thought he might have
died, but—

"Have you come to kill me?" he asked.

"I have come for answers."

He raised his head. "It matters not. I am dying anyway."

"How so?"

"Our skin isn't meant to be wet for this long. I can feel
great sheets of it sliding from my hands."

I swam behind him. The bones of two fingers were
exposed, the flesh quite gone. "Are you not in pain?"

"Do you care?"

"I am curious," I said. "But if you prefer, I will stop being
so. How many ships will Toby Wick have waiting for us?"

"Just one," he answered, wearily.

"A falsehood. Everyone knows he travels in a fleet."

"Every *whale* may know that. Every man knows he travels
in a fleet of one. It's his arrogance. Otherwise, he doesn't consider it a fair hunt."

"These are lies. I will hurt you more, if I must."

"If you *must*," he spat. "Yes, I have heard of your *musts*.

Whales and their precious prophecies. 'We must do this. It has been prophesied.' You relieve yourself of choice. Relieve yourself of consequences. Torture me, harm me, kill me. Do all these things, but do not pretend there is a *must*. That is how evil is rationalized."

This was by far the most he had ever spoken, but I was astonished at more than the length. I knew men studied our culture as we studied theirs, but we prided ourselves on keeping them in ignorance. The top of the sky was *far* too high for them to dive. No man had ever seen a city of ours from more than the greatest distance. They had to guess at what we did there, how we lived, what we believed (much as, it must be said, we had to do with their own great cities on land). And yet, here was this male, this *young* male, speaking of prophecy.

"We are not evil," I said. "We are protecting ourselves."

"I have seen inside your hull. How do our floating heads protect you?"

"How does dumping our skinned carcasses in the sea protect *you*?"

"I never wanted to hunt. I was conscripted. Forced aboard. Taken from my village, beaten so I would agree, imprisoned in the hull when I would not."

I was confused. "Why should this be so? Hunting is primary in your culture. You seek it out as your highest destiny–"

"I have never killed anyone, neither man nor whale. Unlike what you're about to do. How does that make you better than me, Bathsheba? How does that not just make you another rumor of Toby Wick?"

He stopped, his chin dropping to his chest. Only then did I realize he had been without man food for at least a day, nor any of the water they drank with the salt removed. He was right, he *would* die soon.

One of the tales of Captain Alexandra's legend was how she had once chased a man all the way to shore and harpooned him as he stood on his own beach. Her pod had found a ship sinking in a storm and helped to finish the job, scuttling it and harvesting the men. This one man escaped on a launch, the winds carrying him fast away.

How he must have blessed whatever gods he served when he saw the shore. How his heart must have thrilled when he landed not even on rocks, but a beach, the violent ocean spitting him out onto the softness of the sand. He was free, not only of the sinking of the ship, but of the whales he had seen dragging his shipmates to their dooms.

Our Captain had followed him. The water was deeper than most shores, obviously, but still only barely deep enough for a great whale. The legend is that he taunted her from the beach. "I beat you!" he shouted. "I beat you in your own element, you filthy, stinking whale!"

Captain Alexandra launched her harpoon from the water and dragged him back into the ocean's crushing hands.

"Wrong," she whispered before she broke him in half. "I beat you in *yours*."

I frequently imagined that man's face. The outrage, the sense of injustice as he stepped into the arms of freedom only to be yanked back. I imagined his terror as my great Captain spoke the last words he would ever hear.

It was how I always imagined the face of men. Taunting, defeated. It was one of our best ways of dealing with the fear of the hunt.

But now here was this man before me, entirely in my own element, close to death. There had been no taunts. There had been no chase. There had only been fear and sorrow. He looked blearily out to me, and I could tell the depth of the shock that still addled his mind and body. He would be lucky to live out the day.

For a moment, that troubled me. But it could only be the novelty of such close proximity to a man. Even the most senior whales only spoke to one or two men in their entire lifetimes. Yet here I was, a mere Third Apprentice, in full conversation.

Yes, the novelty. It must be that.

"I will bring you fish," I heard myself saying. "They will be raw, but the fluid in them will at least keep you hydrated."

I didn't wait for him to answer, just swam to our Captain to tell her what I'd discovered. ◆

20

"THAT IS A LIE," TREASURE SAID, AS SOON AS I spilled my news. "One ship. Ridiculous. A trap, and only a fool would believe it."

"And why does he yet live?" Willem asked, seeming genuinely curious.

"I believe he knows more than he has said," I explained, but only to the Captain. "I believe he speaks what he thinks to be true, but we might learn valuable more if we keep him talking."

The Captain, staring into the great emptiness ahead of us, said nothing for a long, long moment. The deepness in this part of the sky was too high above for even us to echolocate its limit. Even now, in this modern age, we pondered what it might contain, what other civilizations might lurk in that eternal dark.

"*I* would only have one ship if I were Toby Wick," our Captain finally said.

"The fewer to share any bounty with," Treasure said.

"The fewer to share the *glory* with." The Captain looked back to me. "And you think this young male knows more?"

"I have said I would bring him food," I answered. "I believe he *wishes* to speak and that showing generosity rather than pain will make him do so."

The Captain was thoughtful again. "You may be right. You will kill him, Bathsheba, but not just yet."

I turned to swim back to the mast. "Bathsheba's in love," Treasure taunted as I passed.

"With a man?" Willem giggled, with scandalized pleasure. "How would that even work?"

I left them behind to their nonsense, though my skin felt hot and angry against the water. ◆

21

I WAS ON FIRST WATCH THAT NIGHT, THE sky dark above my head, the Abyss dark below, save for the glimmering, shifting moon that pulled the tides. My species of whale rarely slept fully, when we would hold our bodies vertical in the water, gathered in an almost-prayerful circle for protection, and only then for mere moments. Mostly, we half slept, as now, the Captain, Treasure, Willem, and the sailors swimming slowly in the water, their consciousnesses dipping just below the surface of their waking day. Even Demetrius slept, having finally eaten.

"We don't eat them raw," he had said, after I herded some small fish to him and had his hands unbound.

"Your fire has no place in the ocean. Eat or not. I do not care."

He looked up. "Then why bring them?"

I had no answer.

Now, I swam just beyond the tip of my Captain's great forehead. With our comparative sizes, my slipstream was utterly inadequate to pull her along, but the feel of it was enough for her to follow without waking. The Apprentices and sailors were behind *her*, her slipstream alone enough for them all.

We swam toward the prophesied mountains. I have heard that men navigate by the stars, the small lights that dapple the Abyss around the moon. *We* used the magnetic fields we sensed in the water, but that did not stop the stars from being beautiful. I looked at them when I dipped into the Abyss to refill my breather bubble.

If we could reach the stars, I wondered, could we swim in *those*? Would they hold our weight? Could we swim from one to another, like between mountains in the ocean? There seemed to be none of the great unknown continents upon which men lived, continents whose coasts we knew intimately but whose vast middles contained only guessed-at mysteries.

And the moon? What was that? It moved through the Abyss like a ship. A ship whose face showed no men at all. Was it a place without war? Was it a place where a whale fed a man? Would we be safer there? Could the hunt end forever?

I was pulled out of my pondering when I felt motion to my side. Thinking the Captain was waking, I turned to receive my relief orders, but it wasn't her. It was a shark, little more than a tube with teeth and a malevolent brainlessness. It was one of the blues that followed us, hoping for man scraps, but "followed" is the right word. They were lazy and hardly ever stirred themselves to pass us.

But here was another. And another. They swam past me, past the ship, onward, toward something.

Then I scented the blood in the water. ◆

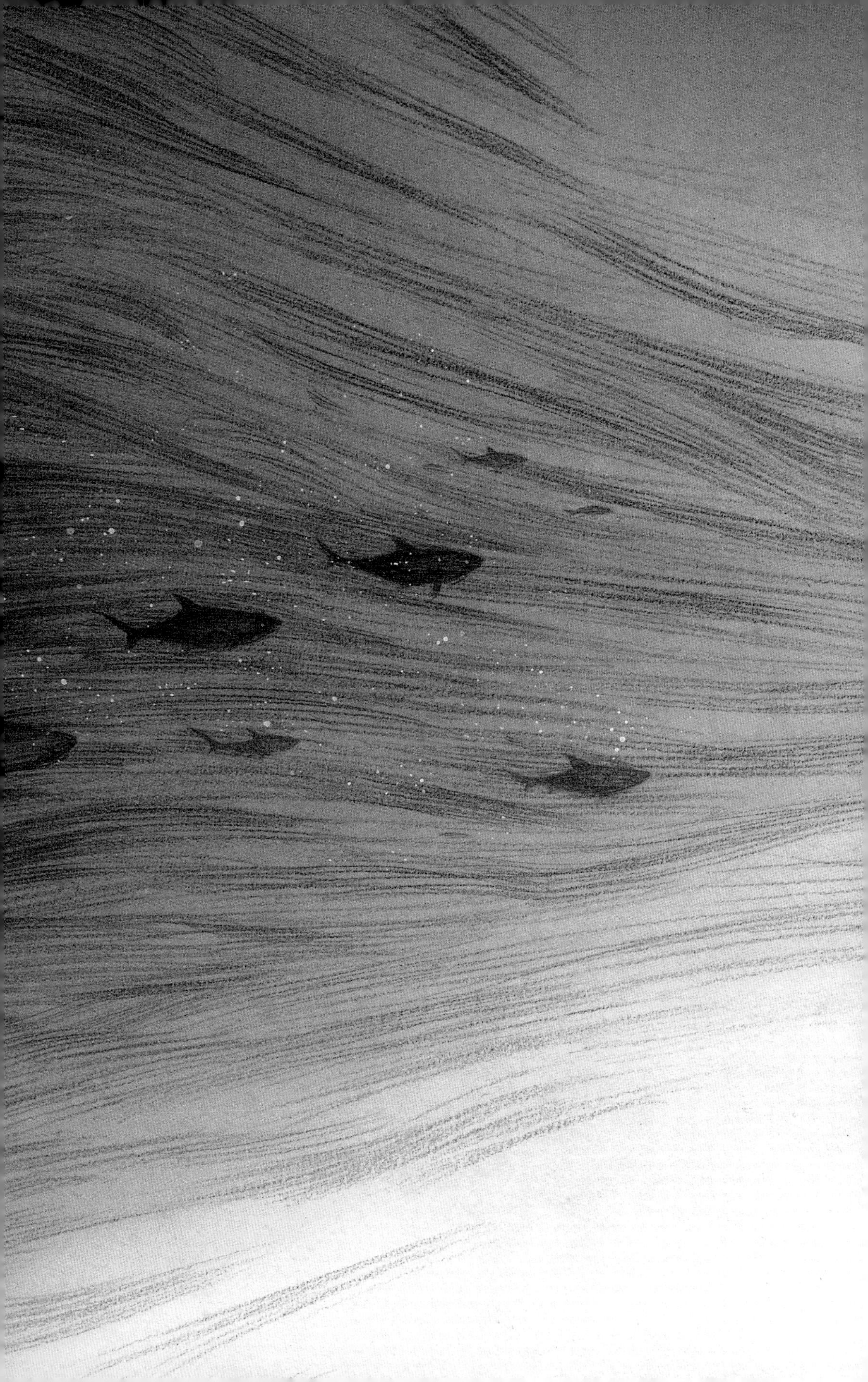

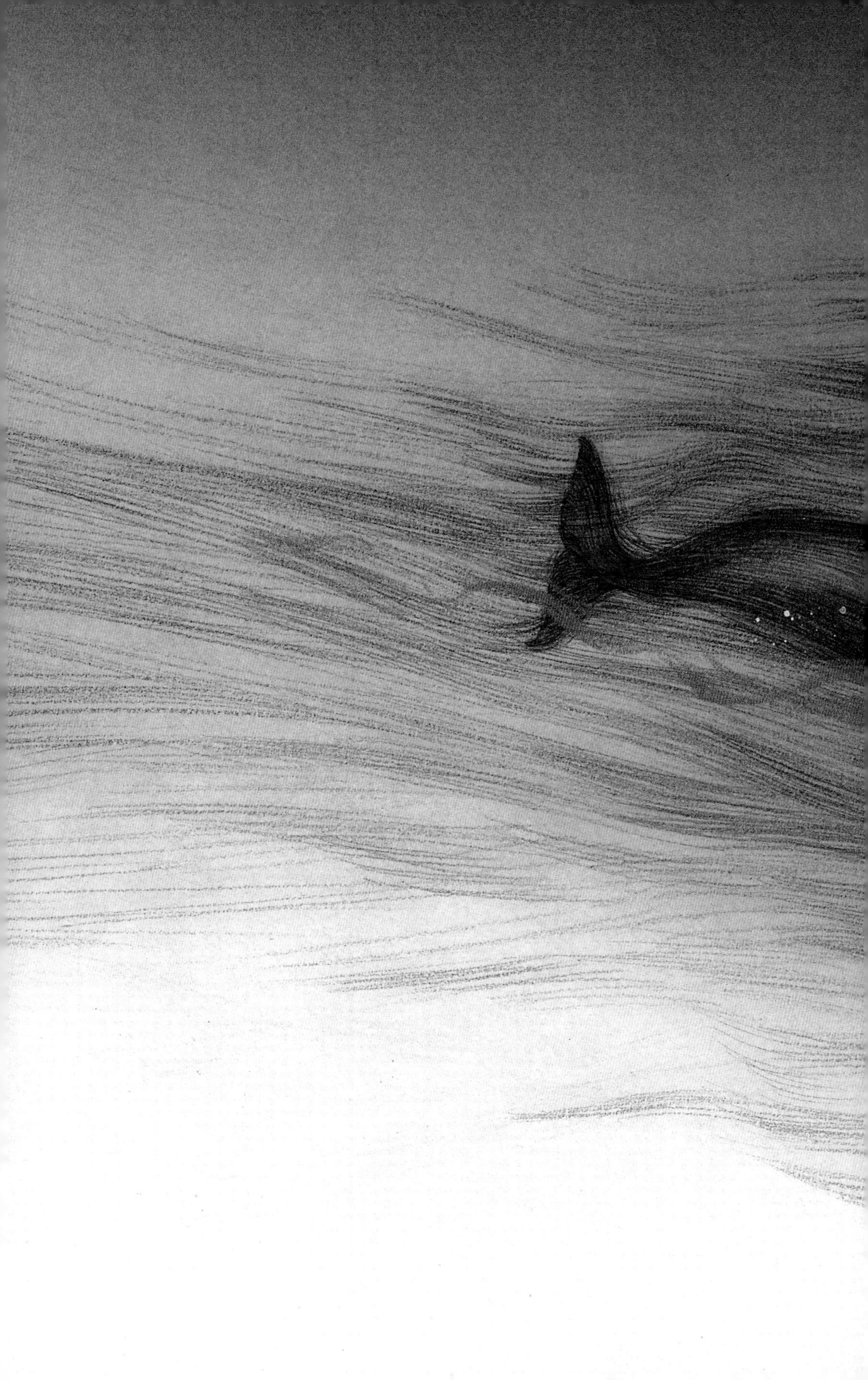

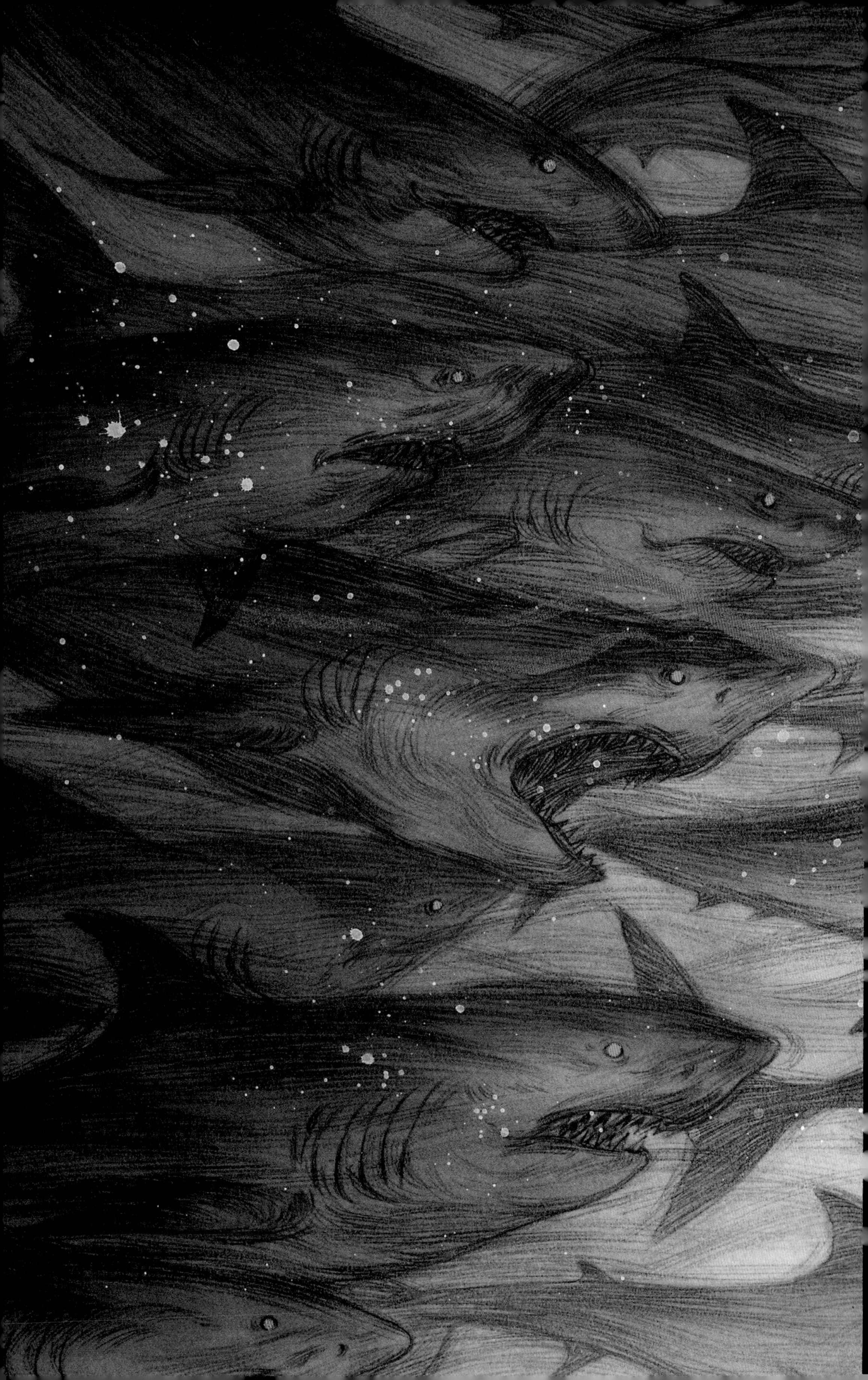

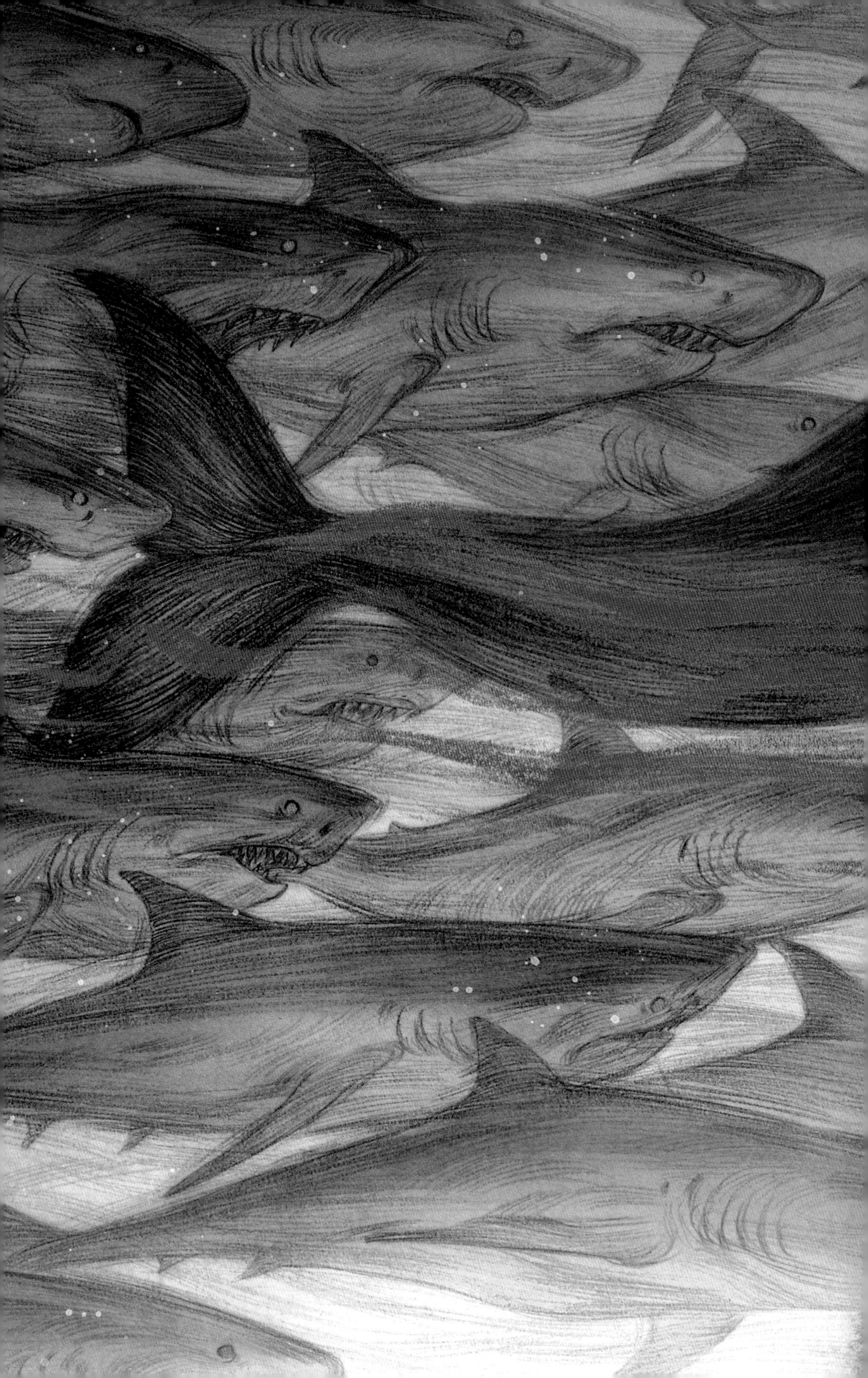

22

"A MASSACRE," TREASURE SAID, STUPIDLY, pointlessly, for it was all there to see.

"But they're intact," said Willem, her eyes wide and fearful. "The hunters have taken nothing from them."

"It is a message," said the Captain.

The night sea ahead of us was darkened by the blood of at least fifty whales, their bodies — yes, intact — bumping against one another. The moon lit them up from below, making shadows against the night.

"How can *all* of them have been hunted?" Treasure asked, fear in her voice. "What *happened* here?"

"It is a message," the Captain repeated. "From Toby Wick."

The float of bodies was starting to quiver as the sharks took their feed. We knew what we had to do, but we were reluctant. We couldn't stop them from eating our dead any more than we could stop the thousands of birds already rising to the under-surface of the Abyss to do the same, but there were personal tokens to gather, families to be informed at a later time, perhaps even salvage and cargo to be rescued. We did not waste.

Unlike men.

"As much as we can," said the Captain. "All of it, if possible."

It wasn't possible. The sharks were too many, eating too fast, and though they skipped out of my way as I approached, the gap behind me swiftly closed again with hungry mouths and blind, stupid eyes. Plus the blood, all the blood, meant we were swimming in a confusing, shifting murk in which even echolocation was of little use. Still, we pressed on.

With my mouth, I gathered mostly coral engravings – our form of identification and how we exchanged money for goods – but also the jewels some of the older generation wore in their scars, adorning them with pride. I gathered small foodstuffs and at least six heater crabs, putting them all in the slings of my harpoon harness. The water grew darker, and so did my mood. I found several defensive harpoons, all unused – all? What *did* happen here? How big was the devil we were chasing? – but there was little time to think. I merely kept gathering, as did the others, trying to reclaim as much as we could before the bloodied and flesh-filled water became intolerable.

Then I came upon the child.

Normally our young were the easiest pickings for the sharks – their size, their vulnerable surprised cluelessness –

but this one was tucked under the fins of her mother, out of immediate sight. I wouldn't have found her myself if I hadn't been recovering another heater crab that turned out to be dead, too. The child was little more than the length of my harpoon, too small to carry anything but the toy starfish she held tightly under her fin.

The mother had clearly tried to protect her, used her own great body to shield her baby from whatever calamity had come from the Abyss. The larger whale had a bloody wound down from her blowhole, already being made larger by twisting sharks, but the little one didn't have a mark on her. Not a single one.

She had drowned. The hardest, most senseless death of all our kind. Not fast, not painless, avoidable as the Abyss was almost always in reach. She had been so afraid to leave her mother that she had allowed her breather bubble to empty and wouldn't go to refill it.

It felt as if something gave way inside me, small, nothing huge or fatal, but a collapse of some internal tissue, near my heart, near my lungs, near the very center where I hid all my hurt and worry.

And anger.

You are thinking I saw my own mother protecting me, and of course, you're right. But I also saw myself as the larger whale protecting my mother. And every whale in turn, again and again, from generations ago to years from now, folded under the fin of another, and another, and another, shielding us from the enemy who would cause a child, the tiniest calf, to drown.

I swam slowly forward, touching her side with my forehead. I let a low wailing keen rise from me, a keen for the calf, for this massacred pod, for myself and all of us here in this eternal war. Whale speech is long and slow, it carries for miles like a current. There can be no match, in this universe or any other, for its expression of grief.

Leaving the starfish with the child — let her take it with her to the hereafter that awaits us all — I turned in the murk but couldn't see far enough to our ship, to the one tied to our mast, a breather bubble that would have saved this little one's life now saving his own.

(*I did not want to be a hunter.*)

Yes, but you are *a hunter nevertheless,* I thought. And you will lead us to Toby Wick, whatever he is, however many men make up his legend.

And you will all perish.

A shark came to feed on the child. I broke its back with my tail and sent it to die in the deep, lonely oblivion. ◆

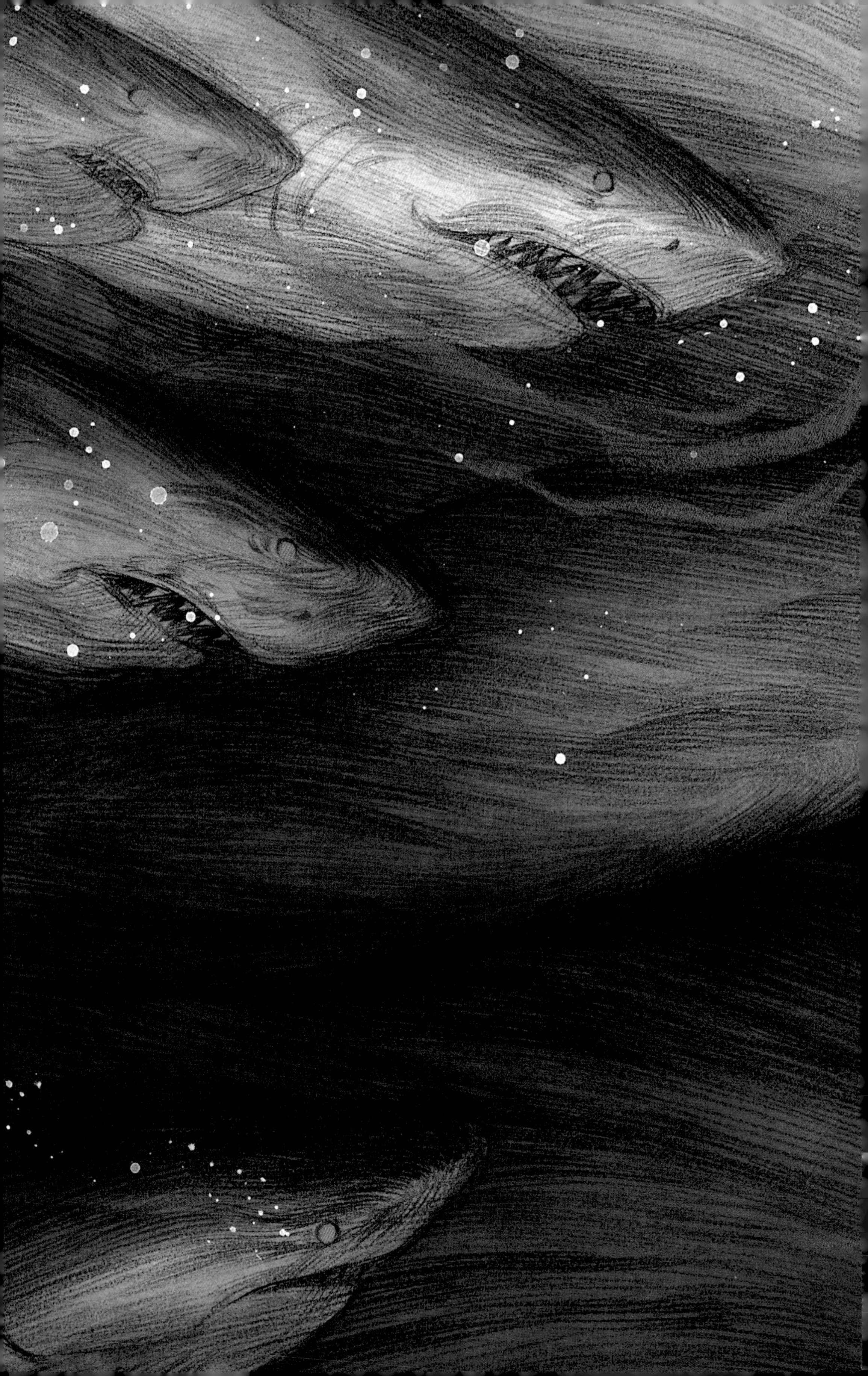

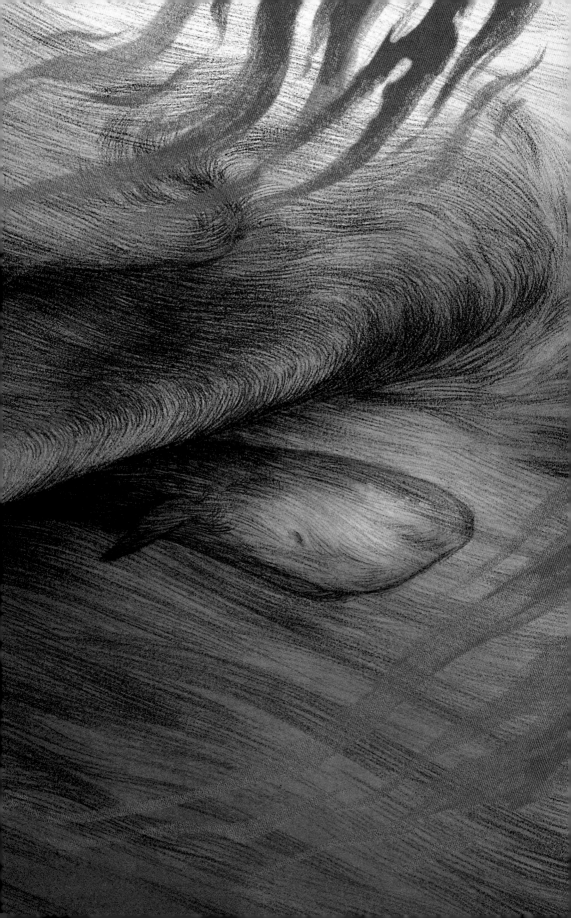

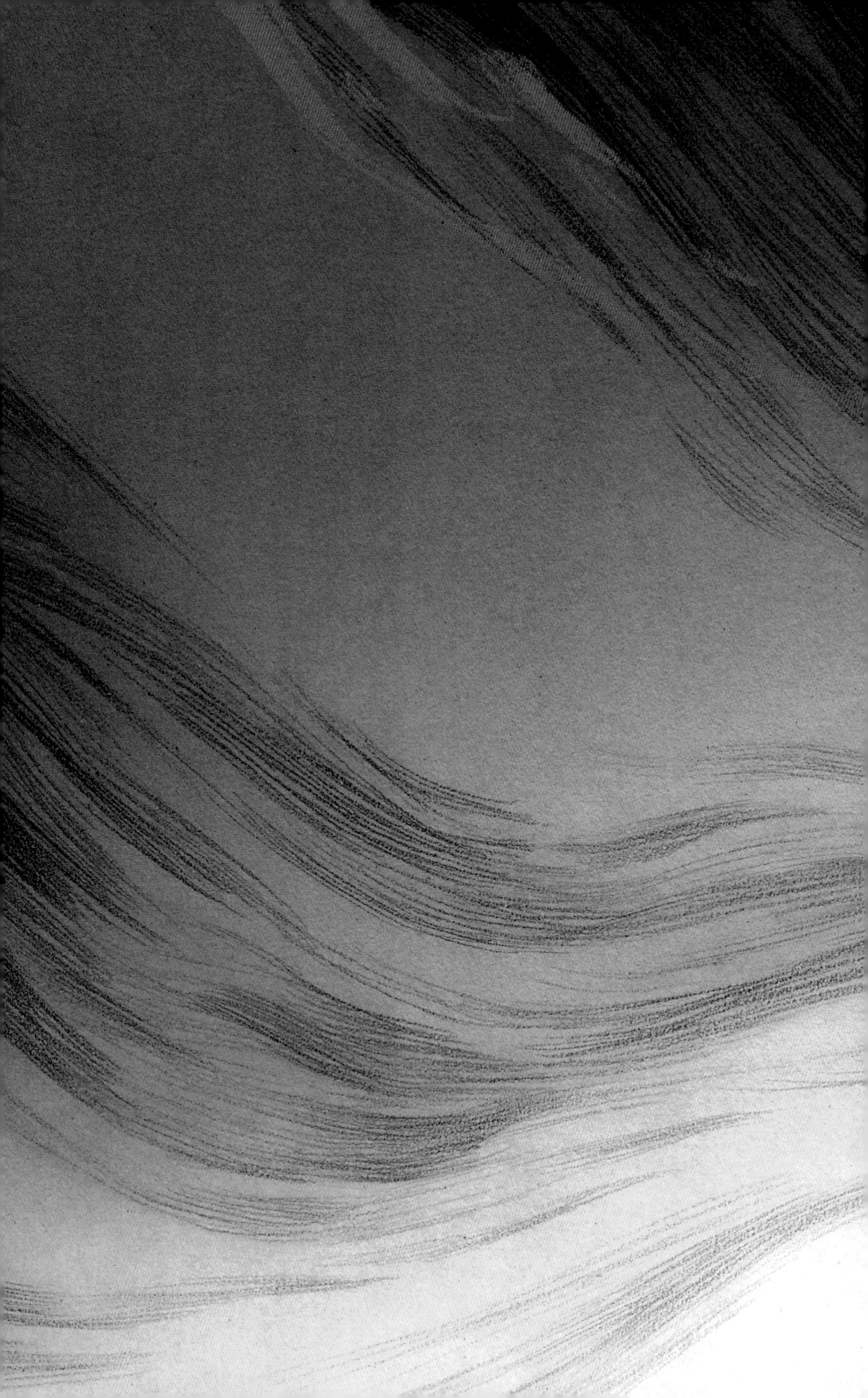

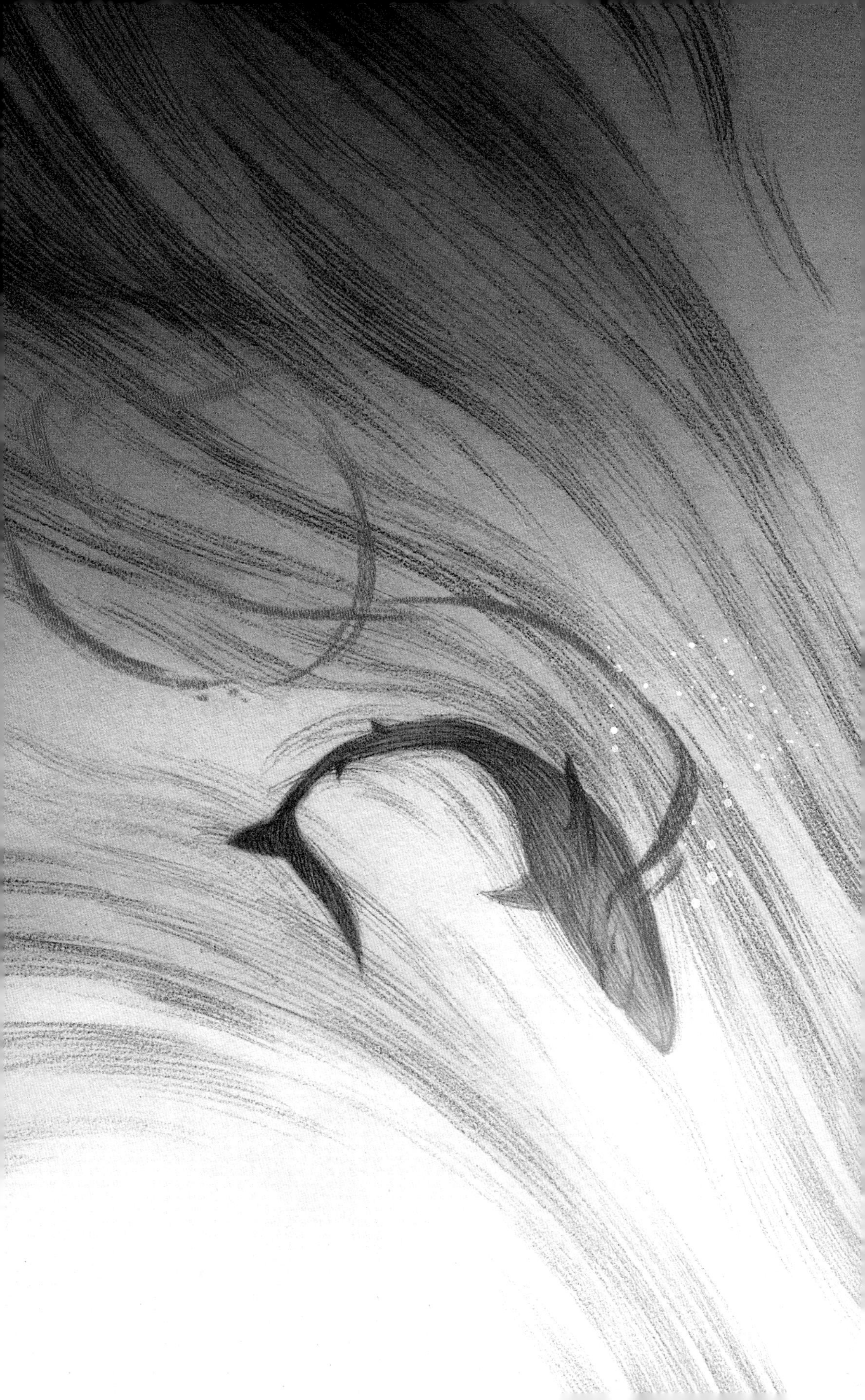

23

"BUT HOW?" I ASKED DEMETRIUS AGAIN, not bothering to conceal my anger. The massacre of the night before had left the thoughts of none of us.

"There is no other answer," he said, pleading. "Only what men tell each other. No one *sees* him. We only say that Toby Wick is a devil. A devil who will do the same to you when you find him."

"You are right that we will find him. You are wrong that he will have a chance."

"You don't see the trap? He waits for the challenge of the whale who will dare to come to *him*. He wants it. And he will be victorious."

"*You* might want it, but *he* will not get it."

"WHAT MAKES YOU THINK I WANT IT?"

And at that, at this flash of impatience, of impertinence from one whose people had killed so many of mine, my own anger overflowed. Without knowing what I was going to do, I blew a breather bubble around his entire body and grabbed him in my mouth again, tearing him away from the mast.

I dove. Up high. And fast. I could feel questioning clicks from Treasure and Willem and even our Captain behind me, but I left them.

"What are you doing?" he panicked. "I won't survive!"

I dove, faster still. The ocean grew dark around us. I kept having to put more air into his breather bubble as the pressure grew, crushing it, trying to crush *him*. The cushion of air around him was the only thing keeping him alive.

The water rushed along my skin as my tail worked, my blood pumping warmth that would only counteract the decreasing temperature for so long. The air in my lungs, too, would also be compressed, that which I wasn't wasting on keeping the young male alive.

"Is this my death?" he shouted, struggling to be heard over the rush of water.

"I want you to see!" I shouted back and dove up and up and up and up and up, past where we usually floated our cities, past where even the brightest sunlight would reach, past where my armor of blubber would keep me from hypothermia for only so long, up and up and up.

Until there was only blackness.

"There is nothing *to* see," he said, his teeth chattering. Even a heater crab wouldn't save him down here. We only had mere moments.

"Here," I said, "in the cold, in the dark. This is where a whale is taught she will see her real self."

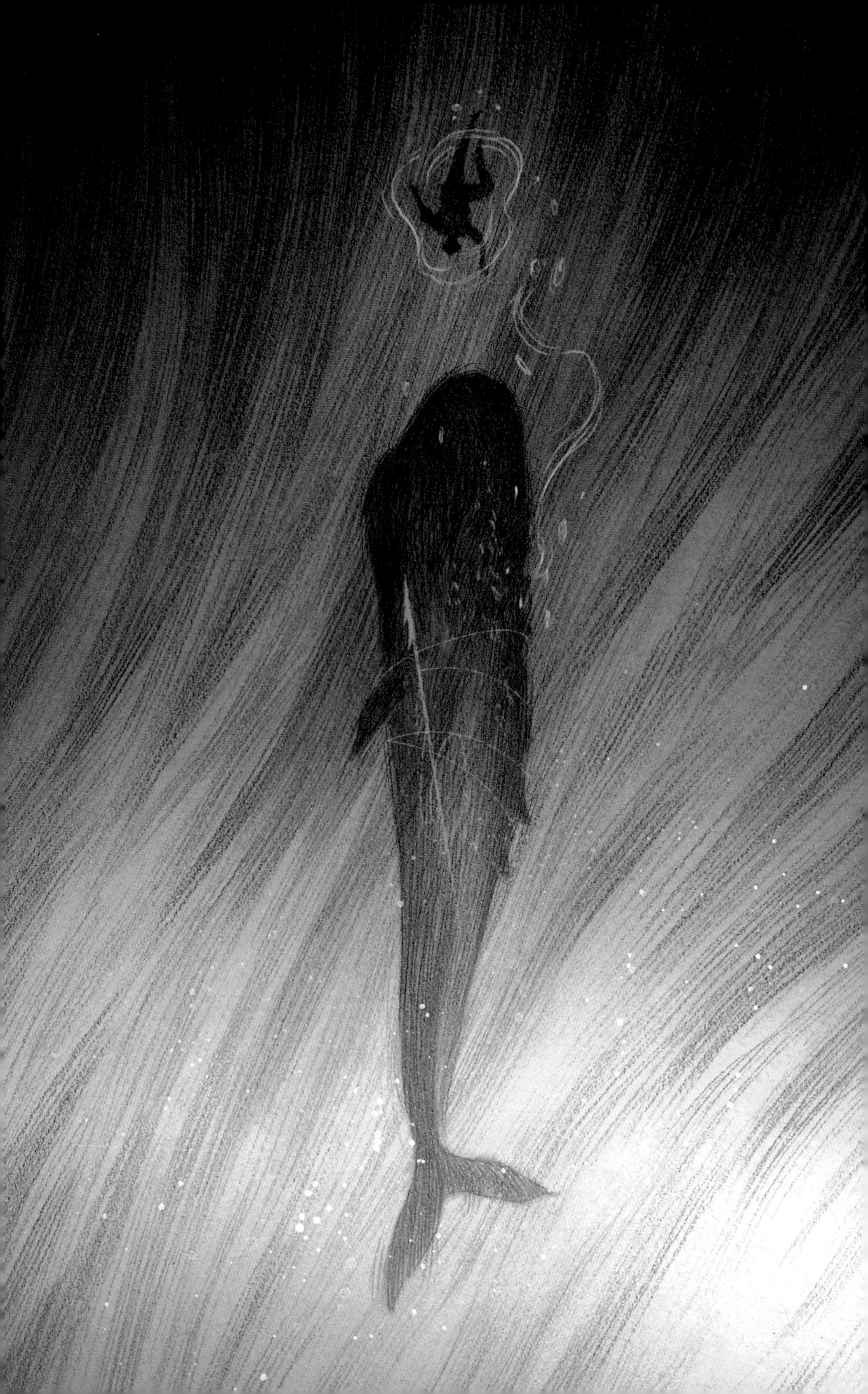

"Your real self is blackness?" he said, confused.

"No, *your* real self is blackness. I can see perfectly well with my echolocation. Leave you alone in the black and you become nothing. You *are* the darkness. But I still see you! I swim in the blackness and I still know who I am, Demetrius!"

I could tell by his silence he was as surprised as I was.

I had used his name.

"You sound like him," he finally said, quietly. "You talk the way *men* talk when they want to emulate him. The way they use his name to do terrible things. If you fight the devil, you become him."

"Maybe it takes a devil to fight a devil," I said.

"But at the end of that fight, Bathsheba," he said, "don't only devils remain?"

And for a moment in the ocean, there was only blackness. We were alone. Even with ourselves.

And whatever devils lurked, unseen. ◆

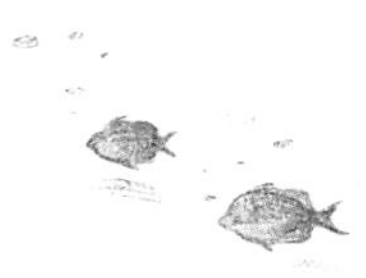

24

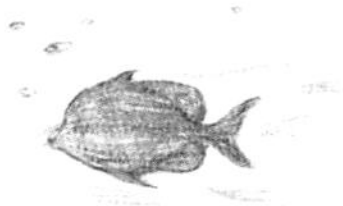

"HE EXPECTS US TO BELIEVE A POD OF FIFTY was killed by a single ship?" the Captain said, rightfully scornful. "By Toby Wick's ship alone?"

"This is what he believes," I answered, ignoring the hostile glare of Treasure and the more thoughtful but still frightened glance of Willem. They had grudgingly accepted my explanation that I had taken Demetrius into the deep sky to frighten him. Though it *had* gone right up to the very, very edge of too much independence in the face of a Captain, which I was sure she would not forget.

"He is also certain we are swimming into a trap," I said. "That we are being led by Toby Wick to our deaths."

"You put a lot of faith in his certainty," the Captain said. "I ask for information, Bathsheba, and you give me opinion."

"Captain—"

"Silence," she said, so quietly and coldly, I was immediately afraid. The sun was passing out of the Abyss, reflecting pinks and yellows across its surface. In the distance, I could see the faint lights of a far-off city, where whales were living their lives, away from the lonely souls who protected them.

"I do not believe we are swimming to suicide," the Captain finally said.

"It was prophesied," Treasure said. "We are the ones who can defeat Toby Wick. That's why he wants us to chase. No other fight is worth the effort."

"I want to hunt this prey as well," I said. "I am merely wondering–"

"You wonder what it costs to kill the devil," the Captain said, fast, harder than I expected, again noticing more than I wished. "You wonder if you would become one yourself."

She suddenly loosed herself from the tow ropes and rounded on me, so fast I couldn't avoid bumping into her. She swam to nearly vertical, her great chest filling the sky above me, forcing me back. Her fins and tail churned to keep her in position, and I could feel the power rolling off her. A current on her own. An ocean I could never hope to navigate.

"Tell me, Bathsheba," her great whale voice booming, stretching through the water, so loud Treasure and Willem had to swim away. I remembered the question Demetrius asked me in the sky. *Is this my death?*

"Do you consider *me* a devil?" my Captain demanded of me, and I felt – I *knew* – that my life depended upon my reply.

She swam closer, pushing me back once again. "Answer!" she commanded.

"Captain–"

"Am I a devil who would kill innocent mothers and babes?"

I believed she might be, but I knew how to answer this one at least. "No, Captain."

"Am I a devil who would lead my Apprentices into hopeless battles?"

Again, I answered contrary to my belief. "You are not."

She turned a great eye to me, wide, her voice the only thing that existed in my world. "No, Bathsheba, that is not why we fight. We fight so that we may *stop* being devils!"

And at this, I could hold back my anger and confusion no longer, even if it killed me. "But what if it's the *fighting* that makes us so?"

Immediately, her great body bent in the water, her tremendous forehead, the rusted harpoon sticking from its scar, moved past me like a tidal wave, her voice dropping to a kindness so sudden, so shocking, I nearly swallowed my breather bubble.

"And there, at last, my dear Third Apprentice," she said, "is the adult question."

Treasure and Willem exchanged glances at the surprising warmth of this, as if I'd just discovered a secret.

It would turn out that I had.

"Let me tell you why I chase Toby Wick," the Captain

said. "Let me tell you why that coin was meant for me to find. Let me tell you why I and this brave pod of mine will be the ones who will end him, once and for all." ◆

25

"IT WAS THE SOUTH SEA," THE CAPTAIN BEGAN. "Not far from where we are going, if our captive tells no lies.

"I was First Apprentice on a hunting ship. The *Velazquez.* You will have heard of it. The great Captain Velazquez, he of the scar that ran from blowhole to tail. He took us from one corner of this world to the other, hunting men of all kinds, taking us through dangers you three calves could barely imagine.

"Now, every sea has its particular hazards, and the south sea's is that it is hot. So hot this one day that we were required to breach into the Abyss in order not to lose consciousness and drown. But breaching, as you know, is the most dangerous of all for a hunter. Still, needs must. We calculated our risk, we waited for an empty sea, then we breached.

"It seems impossible . . .

"No, it *is* impossible, yet I will say it and I will vouch for its truth until my last briny breath.

"We did not see him.

"No echolocation told us there was a ship nearby, none of us Apprentices nor Captain Velazquez himself reported any hulls – white or otherwise – in the water. You will say our senses were dulled by the heat, and you would be correct, but what group of hunting whales would not see a ship on the Abyss on a sunny day?

"And yet.

"The sailors breached. Then the lower two Apprentices, then myself. Oh, how sweet the touch of cool air, like a crisp slap on the skin as the water falls away and for a moment, a few seconds at most, you are in the Abyss, free of our ocean, plunging somehow both downward and upward into the world of men, crossing their barrier, breathing the air around you, not just a small bubble of it. And no sooner have you leapt, then you are falling again, back to your own world, a thief who has stolen just a fragment.

"I crashed back in as we all do. Cooler but dazed, surrounded by wash and foam, swimming up to reorient myself to the proper whale world.

"And so I never actually saw Captain Velazquez formally breach. I saw his tail forcing its way to the surface, but only at the end of his leap. He was a big whale, but strong, the power he could generate, the speeds we would travel.

It was the key to his success. He was the rare full-grown Captain who could breach completely.

"In the churned-up ocean, we held our breaths for the returning crash of our great Captain.

"I am here to tell you that it never came.

"He leapt into the Abyss. He did not return.

"Only his blood. It fell past us in gouts, currents on their own, winding their way up into the ocean sky.

"And there was the great white hull, among us from . . . From nowhere. For how had we not seen it? How had we not echolocated it?

"Toby Wick had our Captain, who I hoped died swiftly at least. Within seconds, harpoons thundered into the water. Our sailors were picked off at once, and the Second Apprentice was struck right through his blowhole, nets already dragging him to the surface before he could even react.

"The Third Apprentice raced to my side, but she was small and I watched as she was plucked from the water in front of me. The whole of her jerked into the Abyss as if by a giant set of jaws.

"I finally returned to my wits and began a great vertical dive. Our ship was lost, my crew dead. I was sure to follow.

"Which was when the harpoon struck me.

"I spun and spun into the ocean, a spiral of blood behind me, but the harpoon would not come free. I was going to bleed to death or die from the shock and then my body, too, would be cut to pieces by the men who'd destroyed my ship and crew.

"It was then that I found myself back at the surface. I thought I had been diving up, deeper into our waters, but somehow, I was on the Abyss, my fins and tail spinning in the air, splashing blood and foam.

"I stopped when the harpoon itself was grabbed. I was pinned to where I was, my head held below the water. I knew that I was going to die. I knew that it would be painful and prolonged and that I would fail to live to avenge my crewmates.

"I waited for death.

"It did not come.

"The end of the harpoon was snapped off, leaving the remainder in my forehead where it still sits today.

"I was released. As I lay in the water, choking on the blood that poured into my throat, I was only able to turn on my side and catch the briefest glimpse of the hull as it sailed away.

"The T and the W etched on the side of it.

"I expected death to claim me, but unconsciousness did instead, the sharks leaving me adrift while they gorged on the other whale remains in the water.

"When I awoke, I was as you see me.

"Alive. A harpoon fragment my permanent scar, embedded so delicately even our own surgeons fear to remove it. I have had to wear it as a reminder.

"Not that I needed one, for I have been unable to echolocate since that day." ◆

26

WE WERE SHOCKED INTO SILENCE, EVEN Treasure, even Willem. Our Captain could not echolocate at all? The great Captain Alexandra, best hunter in the seas, did it all almost blind?

"It is why I call it prophecy," she said. "This was meant to be. I was spared as a challenge. He took away my best weapon and then *dared* me to see if I could still hunt him. I can. And I will." She turned to me again, her voice so low and powerful in the water that the sea itself bent to her words. "I will destroy the devil Toby Wick. Not because he made me a devil, but because he *thinks* he did."

"It is prophesied," Treasure said, wide-eyed, almost as a blessing to herself. Willem quickly did the same. They all looked at me.

"My Captain, I—"

She turned her face back to the great open ocean, one she could no longer track with echoes, one she simply had to see in all its incompleteness and rely on her crew to find the way for her.

Now we knew. We knew why she believed in the prophecy. We knew why she interpreted the disc as she did. We knew why she believed that Toby Wick had chosen her from all the whales in all the oceans.

It was only in my most secret of hearts that I wondered how much truth lay in the prophecy. How much the present had rearranged the past. She had not seen the man himself, after all; she had only seen a ship scratched with his initials. Surely a version of her story had happened, surely there was truth. Even *I* knew how stories grew and changed in the telling and retelling, especially among hunters.

But how much was entering into legend?

And who, in the end, would be destroyed by that legend?

I did not have long to wait. Before the end of that day, we found again the trail of Toby Wick. ◆

27

It was another man ship, but completely upside down. Its hull poked into the Abyss away from us, but the deck and mast of it, sails and all, were underwater, a perverse flipping of their world into ours.

It felt almost an obscenity.

The ship was seemingly wholly intact. No damage, no holes in the side, no wreckage to indicate how it had tipped. It was merely a whole abandoned ship, waiting for us.

"It seems empty," Treasure said, after our third surveillance pass.

"They would drown," Willem said.

"Obviously, there's no crew," I said.

"There must be air in the hull," said our suspicious Captain. "Otherwise it would not keep to the Abyss." She turned to me. "And what does the captive say?"

"He says he does not know."

"Then perhaps, Third Apprentice, his usefulness is at an end." She swam closer to the ship, looking for further signs, an explanation, anything.

I understood the command I had been given. But my own strange reluctance, which I barely allowed even *myself* to look at, was no match for my fear of Captain Alexandra. I returned to

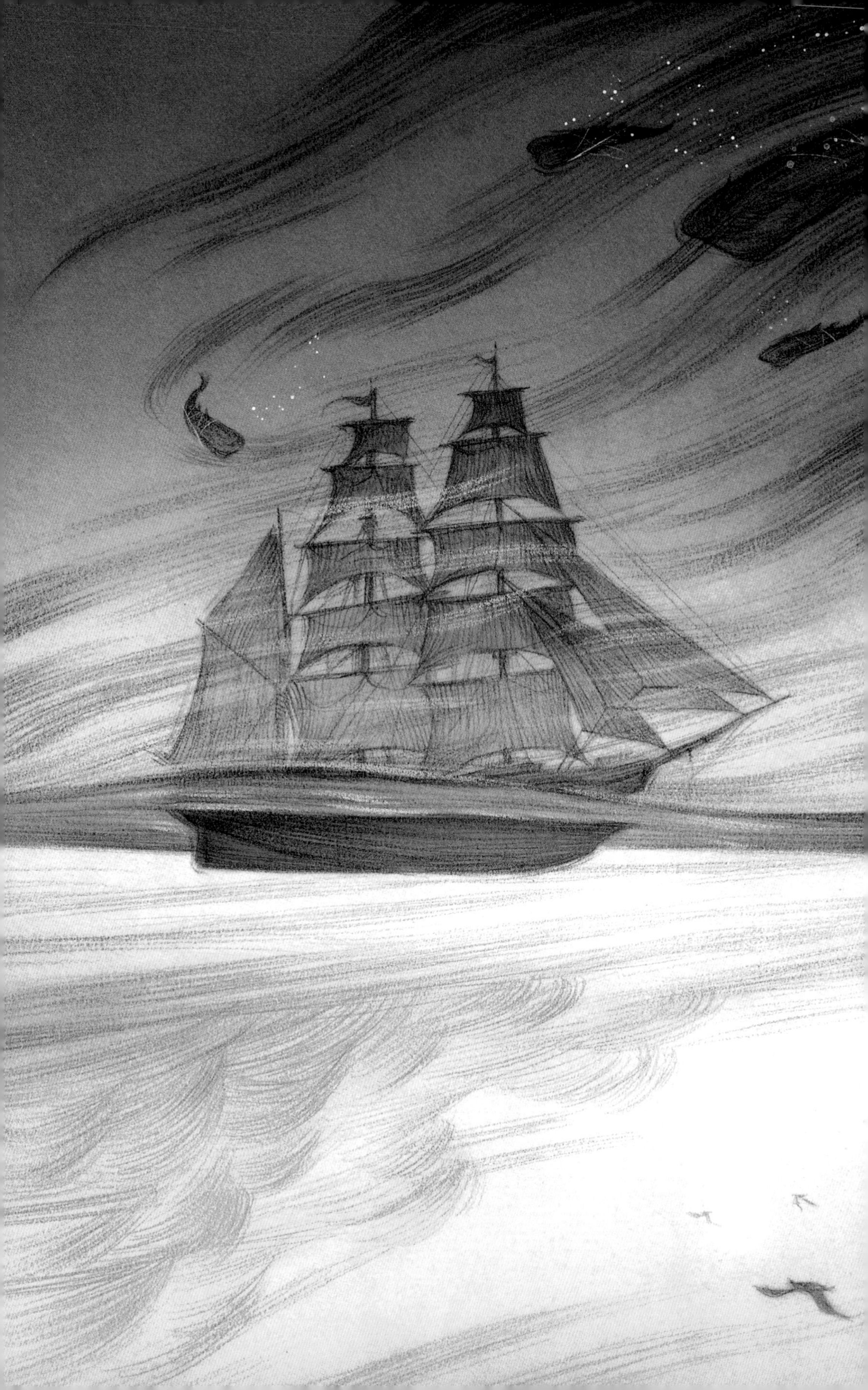

the ever-sicklier Demetrius and had already begun telling myself it was to end his suffering.

Because it was, wasn't it?

"You do not know?" I asked him again. "You are sure?"

"If I knew," he said, "I would tell you."

"Perhaps you are only claiming not to know to hasten your death."

"It is a funny kind of torture where death is the only option either way. The only relief."

I swam around him silently, circling. He was right. What had I offered? Death if he told us the truth, death again if he lied. Where was the threat?

And why *was* I keeping him alive?

"I do not wish to kill you," I said, surprising myself by saying it out loud, though quietly, for only Demetrius to hear.

"That much is obvious," he said, though not happily. "You have let me live far beyond kindness out of your own fear." He dropped his head. "But you *will* kill me. Before the end. And nothing between whale and man will ever change."

I breathed from the bubble in my throat. There was no further delay I could make. He said he did not know what the upside-down ship meant, so he was right:

I would kill him.

And that would be the end. So many ends.

I tried to remember the calf who drowned. I brought her to mind to make it easier for myself—

But he looked so pathetic. So weak. So unlike a man who would strike at *any* whale. Had I found him? Had I truly found the man who wouldn't hunt?

I hovered in the water, a hesitation that would be noticed before long.

"There's a way in!" Treasure shouted from near the surface. She swam excitedly back to our ship. "A hole, just behind the mast, big enough for an Apprentice. Hidden, but clearly meant for us to find." She looked at the Captain. "It's another test, another sign."

"Surely it is that," the Captain said. "But what kind?"

"I will find out," Treasure said. "If you command it. I would go anywhere for my Captain. It is prophesied."

"Swim in, then," said the Captain, barely acknowledging her loyalty. "Touch nothing."

Treasure looked thrilled, shooting us her most arrogant look, before turning tail and swimming ferociously back to the ship. We watched, even Demetrius, as she found the hole she described and disappeared inside.

"Is she going to die in there?" Willem whispered to me.

"She thinks she's fulfilling prophecy," I said.

"Sometimes it's prophesied that you die."

"What do you see?" the Captain called out.

"It is empty," Treasure said, baffled. "Just an empty hull, stripped of all its decks, stripped of almost everything. But wait."

"What do you see?" the Captain said again. "Treasure?"

"There is a box," Treasure said. "A square in an air bubble at the very top – or bottom, I suppose – of the hull, just out of the water."

"Is there a sign on it?" the Captain said, urgently.

"It is hard to get close . . . *Yes!*" she said, her voice exultant. "The same three mountains, the same letters, T and W."

The Captain looked pleased, her great bulk seeming to swell in the current.

"And . . ." Treasure said.

The Captain perked up. "And what? Treasure? What do you see?"

"A setting sun," Treasure's voice came, still muffled by the hull, but her triumph growing. "He will meet us at the setting of the sun."

"Are you sure?"

"I will bring it to you," Treasure said.

"No," the Captain said. "Treasure, wait, I order you to–"

But Treasure must have reached into the air and grabbed it with her mouth. Because the ship exploded. ◆

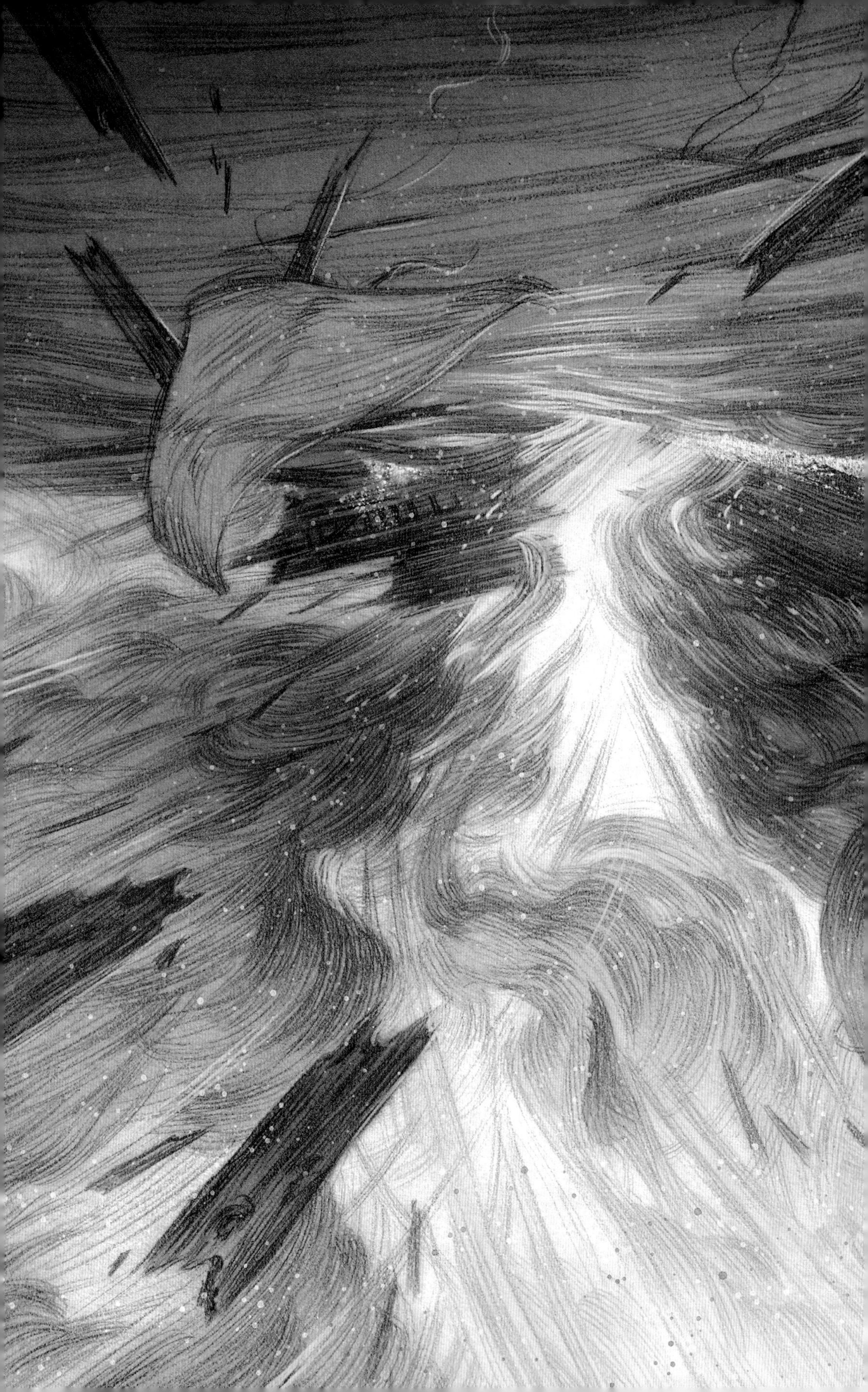

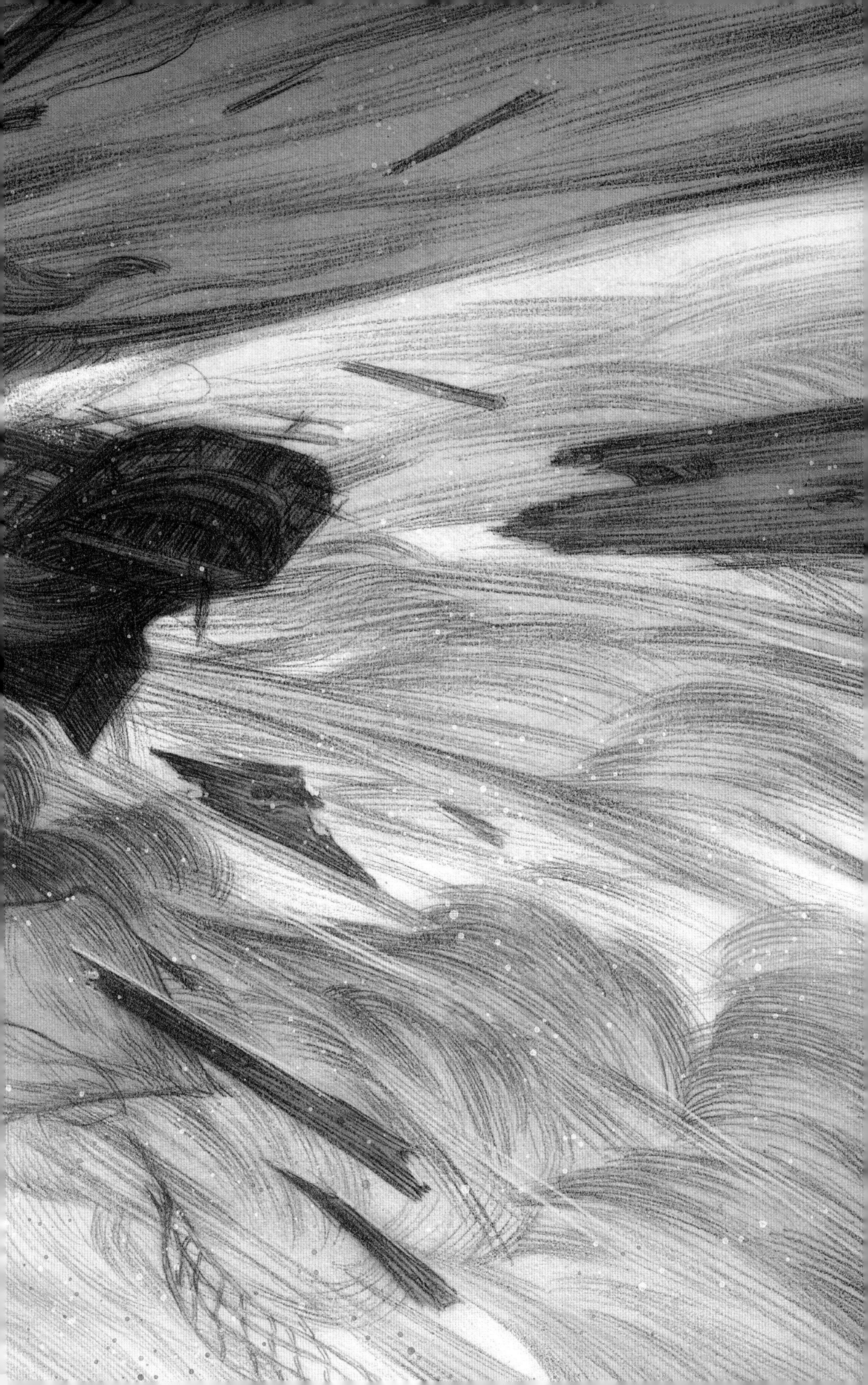

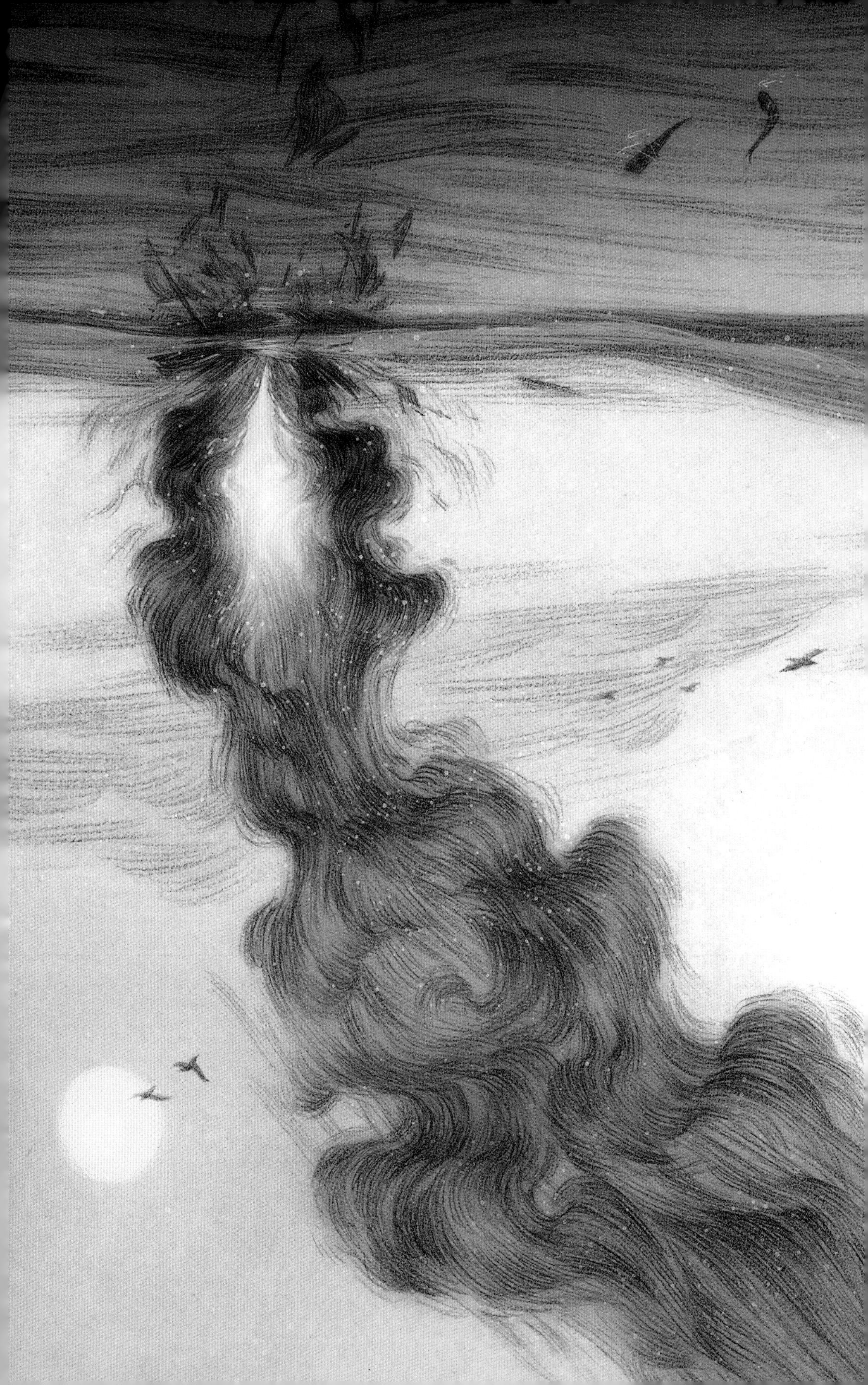

28

MOST OF THE FORCE OF THE EXPLOSION went out into the Abyss, of course — water being a far better barrier than feeble air — but the ocean around us still lurched violently in the shock wave. Foam and bubbles shot past us, trailing from boards shuttling fatally fast. It was only a fluke no one was struck, especially a whale the size of our Captain, though many of the boards did impale themselves into the side of the *Alexandra*.

"Treasure?" Willem asked before the ruptures in the water even ceased. Her eyes wide with panic. "Treasure!"

"Gone," said the Captain. "As prophesied."

"Prophesied by who?" I shouted.

The Captain frowned at me. "It was clearly meant to happen. She knew it. I knew it. This was meant to be."

"Was it?" asked a distraught Willem.

Angrily, I swam through the still-churning wreckage, Willem following close, but it was clear that nothing survived. All we found was a faint pink cloud of blood and pulverized flesh that had once been our irritating and proud First Apprentice.

"She's gone," Willem whispered to me.

I turned on the Captain. "I recall no prophecy that Treasure would die."

"Then that is your own ignorance," the Captain snapped. "Everything is prophecy. Every action in life is meant to happen. Toby Wick was meant to find us. Treasure was meant to sacrifice herself for this message. Even you, doubting Bathsheba, you are meant to be here. And we, the remaining crew, are meant to find and defeat Toby Wick."

I could feel my anger flailing and was unable to hold it in. "Says *who*? You want revenge and are only seeing the prophecy that will allow it."

"Then the question must be asked, Bathsheba," the Captain said. "Why aren't *you* seeing the same prophecy? Your shipmate is dead. A brave convoy of whales is dead. Your own mother is *dead*. Is your universe really so meaningless?"

"Is yours only filled with meaning that will bring more death? That will bring more war?"

And then she *did* strike me with her tail, hard enough to make the blood flow from my mouth.

"You foolish child," she said, almost pityingly. "I see the entire trail of prophecy that has led us here. But that prophecy leads us to the *end* of war, Bathsheba. The end of Toby Wick. An end *I* will bring. An end you will *help* bring. Or I swear to you, I will bring your death myself."

"I see we find you again down one Apprentice," said a voice, from across the water.

Captain Arcturus and his ship swam toward us, menace in his voice mixed with delight. ◆

29

"We heard the explosion," he said. He and his three Apprentices swam in a wide formation that could have been a prelude to surrounding us, if one wanted to read it that way.

"You were obviously close enough," Captain Alexandra said, turning her side to him as she did, the oldest whale warning in the book: never forget how large I am.

"We heard strange languages under the water," he said, looking over to Demetrius, forlorn in his bubble. "And we wondered if a pod was in trouble."

"We need no assistance," our Captain said. "Thank you."

"Yet a ship has been destroyed, along with" —he sniffed the blood in the water— "one of your Apprentices, it seems. And you have a man tied to your mast." His voice took on a smile. "Surely there is *some* help here that another pod can provide."

I saw Willem had taken up a defensive position apart from our Captain. Then I saw I had unconsciously done the same.

"I have neither time nor patience for this, Captain," Captain Alexandra said. "State your business, make your attack, or leave us."

"Attack?" Captain Arcturus said, all innocent. "Now, why would I do that?"

Before he had even finished his question, our Captain was in motion.

With a speed I'd never seen even *her* achieve, she shot toward him through the water, so fast she left a wake that bounced me to the side. Like a living, giant harpoon, she flew at Captain Arcturus, mouth open, teeth bared, tail churning the ocean like the explosion from moments before.

He had no time to prepare. She hit him under the jaw, taking it in her own, forcing him up and back, his blood already in the water as she slammed him into the hull of his ship. The impact was so hard the ship itself heaved and, shockingly, it cracked, a section of it caving under the force of our Captain — our terrifying, powerful Captain — pushing theirs into his own ship.

"Do *not!*" I heard Willem say, swimming fast between the *Arcturus* Apprentices and our Captains. They were turning to attack, but I swam there fast, too. Though we were but two

and they were three, they still hesitated at our ferocity.

I don't know what I was feeling. I was merely responding. Our Captain had made a move, and though just seconds before I was fighting with her, here I was, defending her. Why? Because of her obvious power? Because of her righteous anger at an interloping pod trying to take advantage of our shock and grief? Certainly not because of prophecy woven from thin water to explain any and all events.

Yet here I was.

"We outnumber you," their First Apprentice said.

"We will still fight you," Willem said.

"And we will beat you," I added. "Like our Captain is beating yours."

Indeed she was. She drove Captain Arcturus further into the crushed hull of the ship that bore his name. He struggled mightily with his tail, but our Captain was bigger, stronger. She held him there.

Until finally.

"Mercy!" he cried. "I ask for mercy."

She let him go instantly.

But of course, no whale who has begged for mercy in a fight is ever really let go. It would follow him to the end of his days, however many they were to be numbered.

We had triumphed. ◆

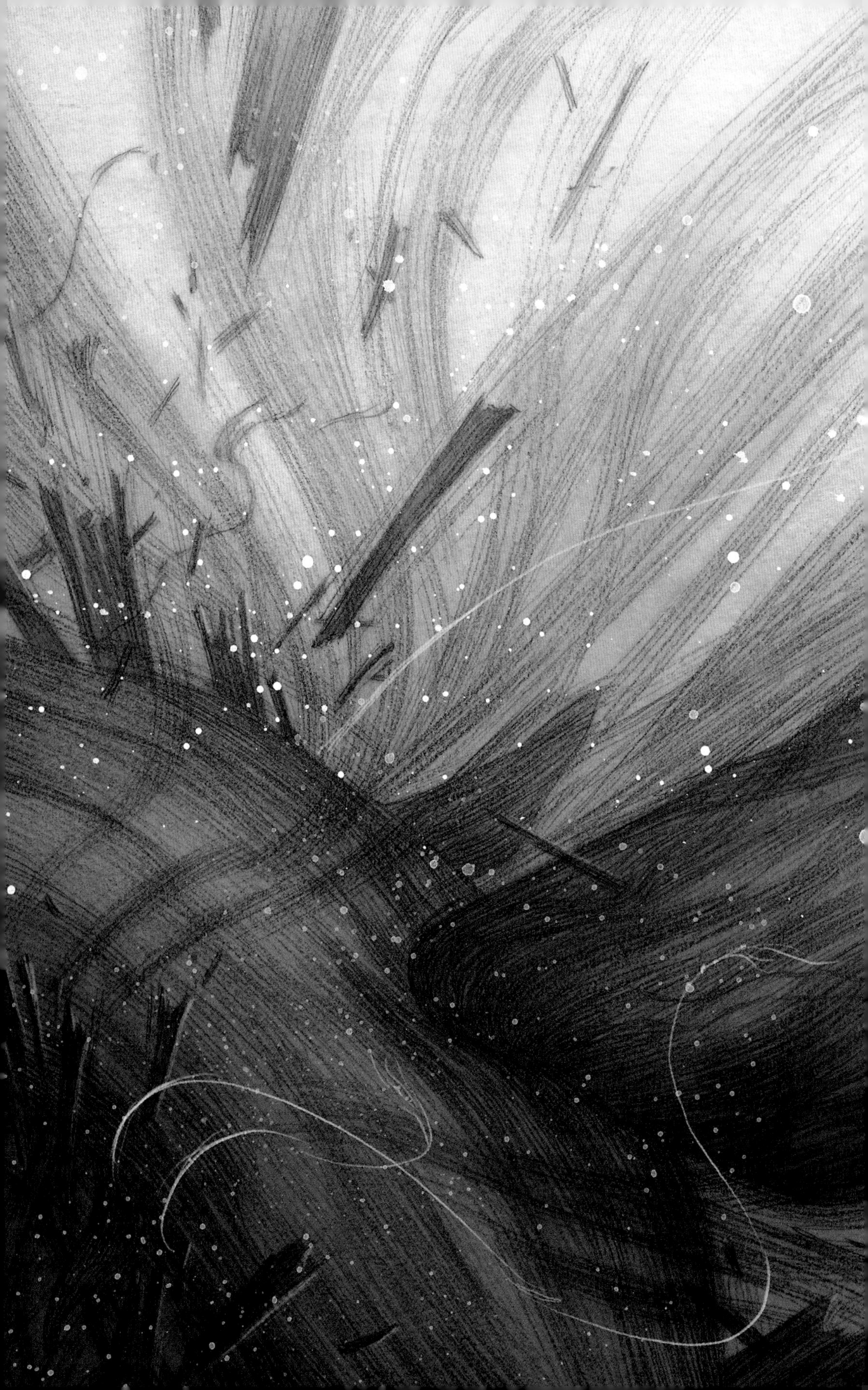

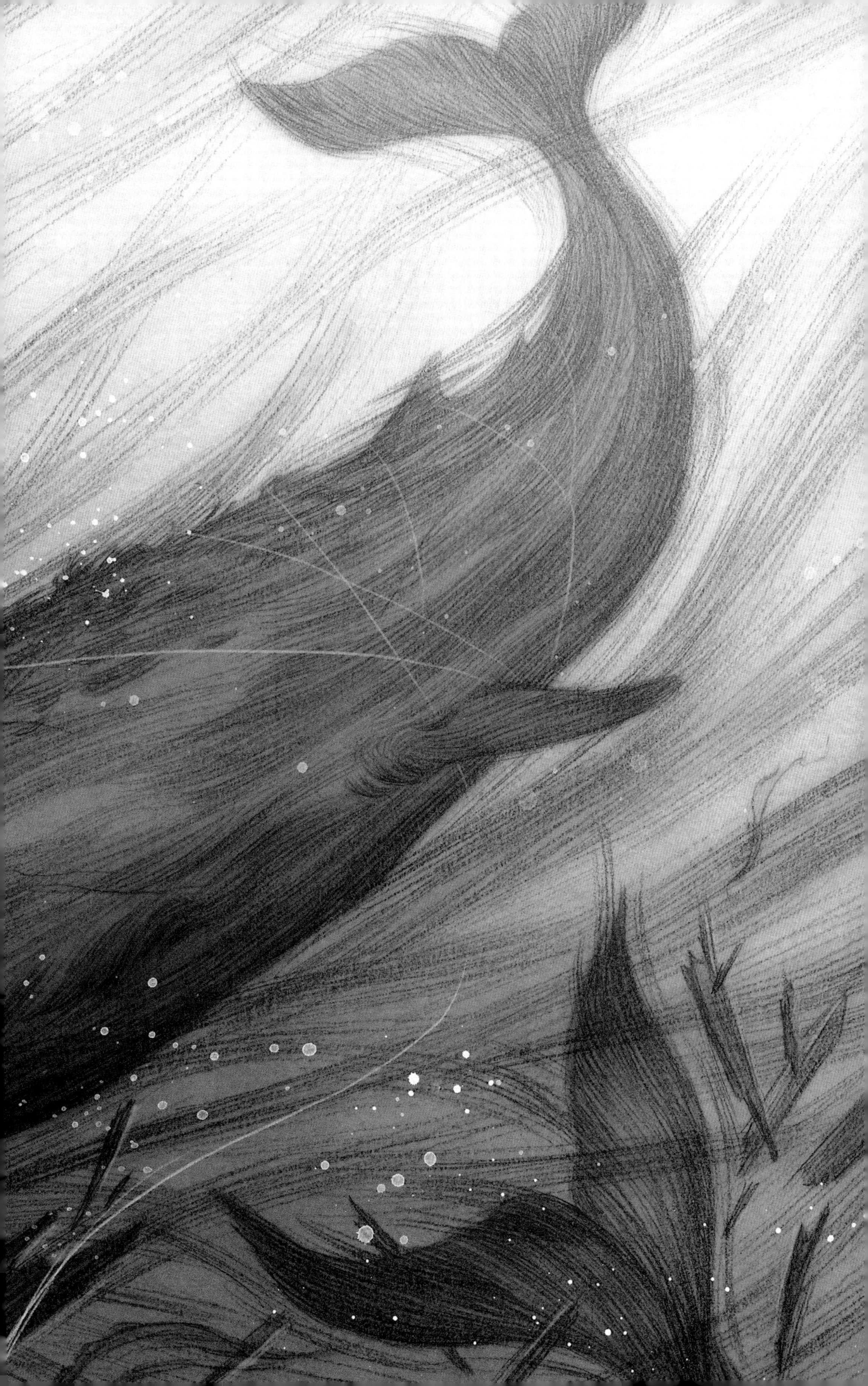

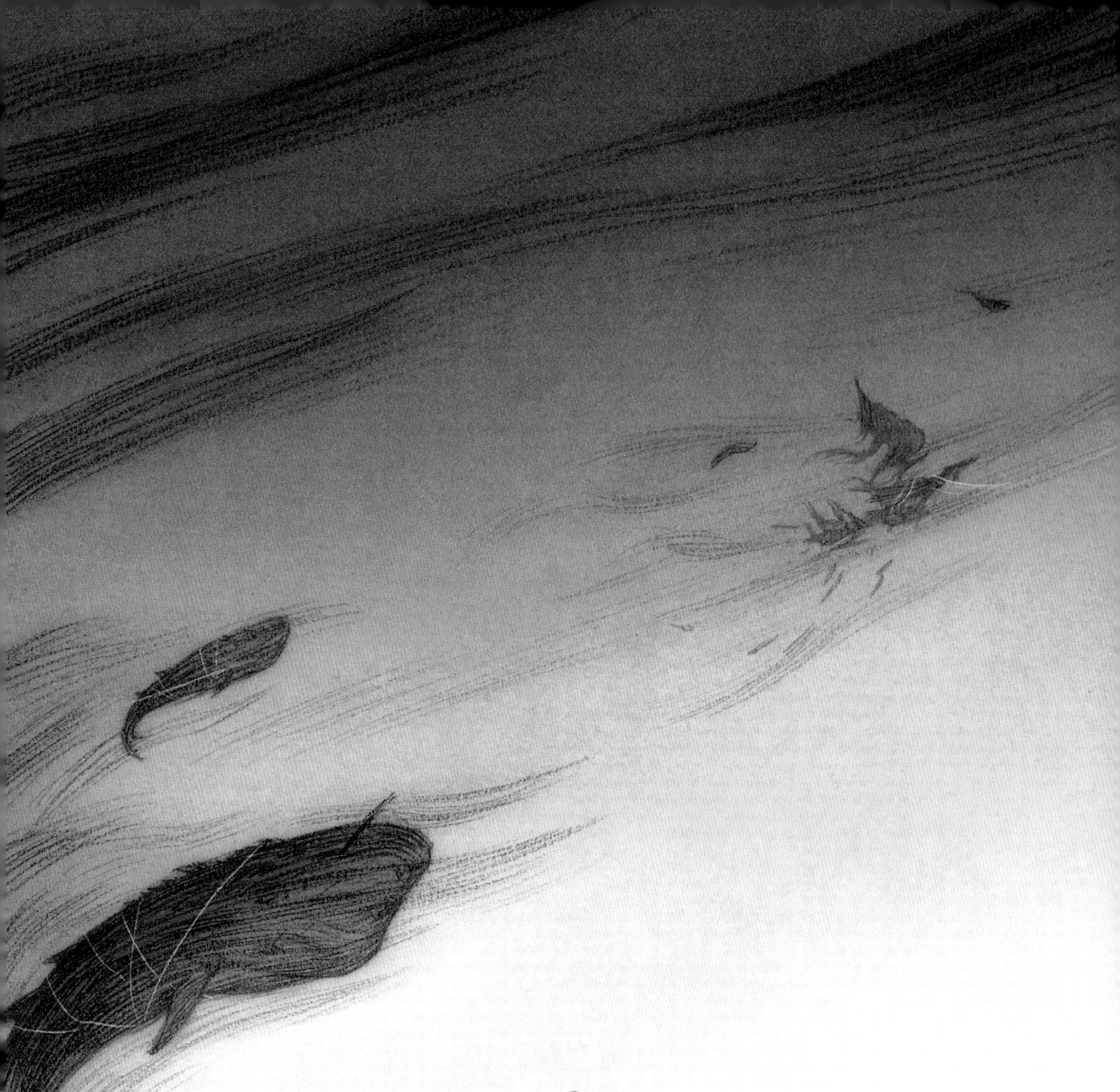

30

As the *Arcturus* pod swam away – for its last time, as no Apprentice would stay with a Captain who cried "mercy"; *I* wouldn't, even Willem wouldn't – our Captain turned, ignoring the superficial wounds she'd received, saying only one thing:

"It is time to meet Toby Wick." ◆

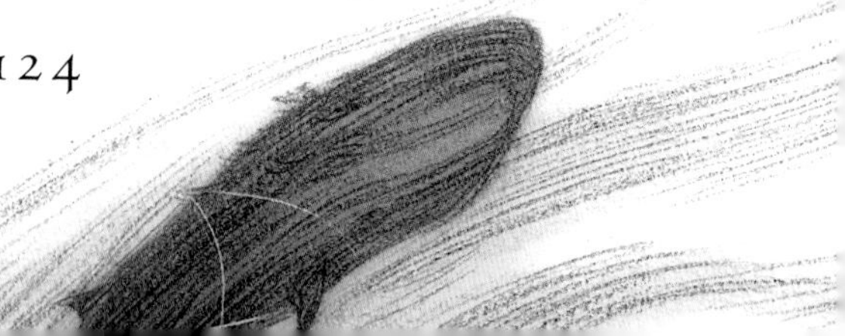

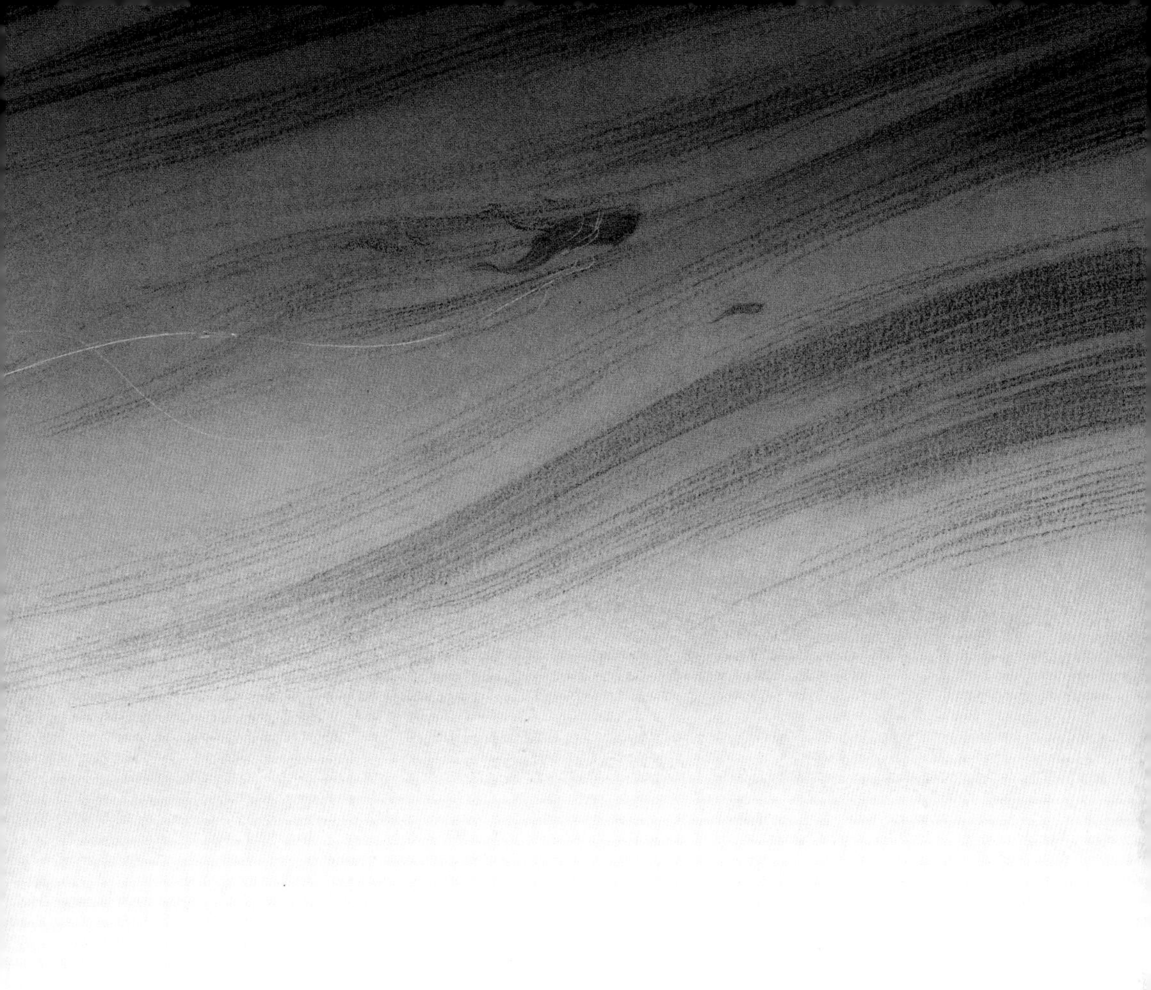

31

"WHICH DAY OF THE SETTING SUN?" THE Captain told me to ask Demetrius. "If he knows, tell him you will end his suffering the moment his words are proven true. If not, kill him now."

I swam immediately to him. "She says—"

"I heard." He caught my eye. "The irony. I finally understand the voices of whales just as they are speaking of my death."

I hesitated. I barely knew the words that were tumbling through my brain and out of my mouth, but here they were. "It is three islands," I said, quietly. "In the confusion, you may swim to one. Tell me. I will not kill you."

"You do not even know your own mind," he said.

"Has there not been enough death?" My brain was churning with all that had happened in such a short space of time, but it was this thought that it kept returning to. And what Demetrius – frail, little Demetrius – had said about sounding like Toby Wick. What sort of life Demetrius might have had in the world of men was beyond me. I had never asked. To me, all men were hunters, but if he *had* been conscripted, forced, and refused, then what did that mean?

What did that mean?

"Has there not been enough death?" I said again.

"Of the other whale? Death is suddenly objectionable to you when the dead has a name you know?"

I swam straight up to him at that, hitting the mast above his head, making him cower. "My mother was killed by a man. Do not presume to teach me of the objectionableness of death."

"I say again, you do not know your own mind."

"What were you before?"

He blinked at me, confused.

"Before you were taken. Before you ended up here. What were you?"

"I . . . was a *baker*," he said, still confused.

"What is a baker?"

"Breads. And cakes." He saw my confusion. These were clearly not things that would last under the water. "I prepared a certain kind of food."

I swam close to him again. "Then know this, Demetrius the baker," I said. "Death is coming. Death I cannot prevent. Large and multiple. But there is one life, perhaps, that I can save. And surely *that* is how the war ends. Not in cataclysm. But in the small saving of a life. I may not know my own mind, but I know that I will not become a devil."

He watched me closely now as I swam in increasingly agitated circles. The Captain was waiting. She would not wait much longer.

"Tomorrow," he finally said. "Tomorrow. At the setting of the sun."

"You knew," I said, so quietly it was almost a whisper. "All this time, you knew."

He just whispered back, "I did not wish to send you to your death, Bathsheba."

And though it may have only been the sun setting, one more time, the ocean felt all of a blackness around me. ◆

32

I TOLD MY CAPTAIN WHAT HE'D SAID, AND we swam through the night, the Captain and her two Apprentices, our sailors tending the ship that bore her name. We were heading to battle, and under-whaled at that. Sailors were never promoted to Apprentices – the skills were different; sailors took such pride in theirs that they scorned ours – but even if they had been, what could one learn in a single night?

We swam with harpoons harnessed to our bodies.

Yes. We were heading to battle.

Demetrius was right. I did not know my own mind. I still didn't know why I said I would spare him, though perhaps he was so ill now that his death was inevitable anyway. How could I know? The biology of men was a mystery to me.

But could I kill him? Though men had been the death of my mother, the death of Treasure, the death of count-less whales . . .

This man had not. And we had both wished to save the other.

I did not know my own mind. It would be my death if I did not solve it.

"Your thoughts should be with us," Willem said, at my side. "Or are they with Treasure?"

"To be truthful, I am not sure where they lie."

"And I the same. I am shocked by her loss more than that of an entire pod. Is that wrong, do you suppose?"

"She was larger in your world than that pod. It's only understandable."

"Thoughtful as ever, Bathsheba."

This caught my attention. Willem had always been so happy-go-lucky, so off in her own little world, so — I hate to say it — dim. Loyal, but always an Apprentice, never a Captain.

"What do you mean?" I asked.

"You notice what the others don't."

"*Maybe* I do."

"Doesn't mean you're right, though."

"No. But I begin to wonder if doubt is better than the wrong knowledge."

She just glanced at me. "I will fight when we get there. I will help the Captain kill Toby Wick. I will do this as First Apprentice. And you, Bathsheba, you will assist us as Second."

It took a moment before I realized what was happening. Willem was commanding me. Before I could even answer, she swam ahead, drafting in the wake of our Captain for a period of relative rest. I stayed in my position, behind them but before the ship.

Where the Second Apprentice always swam.

For Willem was right. We had both moved up a spot. And the Second Apprentice followed the orders of the First Apprentice. ◆

33

I WOULD LIKE TO SAY THAT OUR APPROACH to the three mountains that night was dramatic, that we swam through much peril and reached them just in time to enjoin the battle and win the day.

In truth, we got there early.

They were lone mountains in the deep, far from any others, hanging from our sky and piercing the Abyss, as if the sea had gods and here were three. The current bent around them, but the ocean — which should have teemed with life — was strangely empty.

Including of our prey.

"He is not here," the Captain said angrily.

To my surprise, Demetrius answered her directly. "I can only repeat what was told me by a frightened Captain. Toby

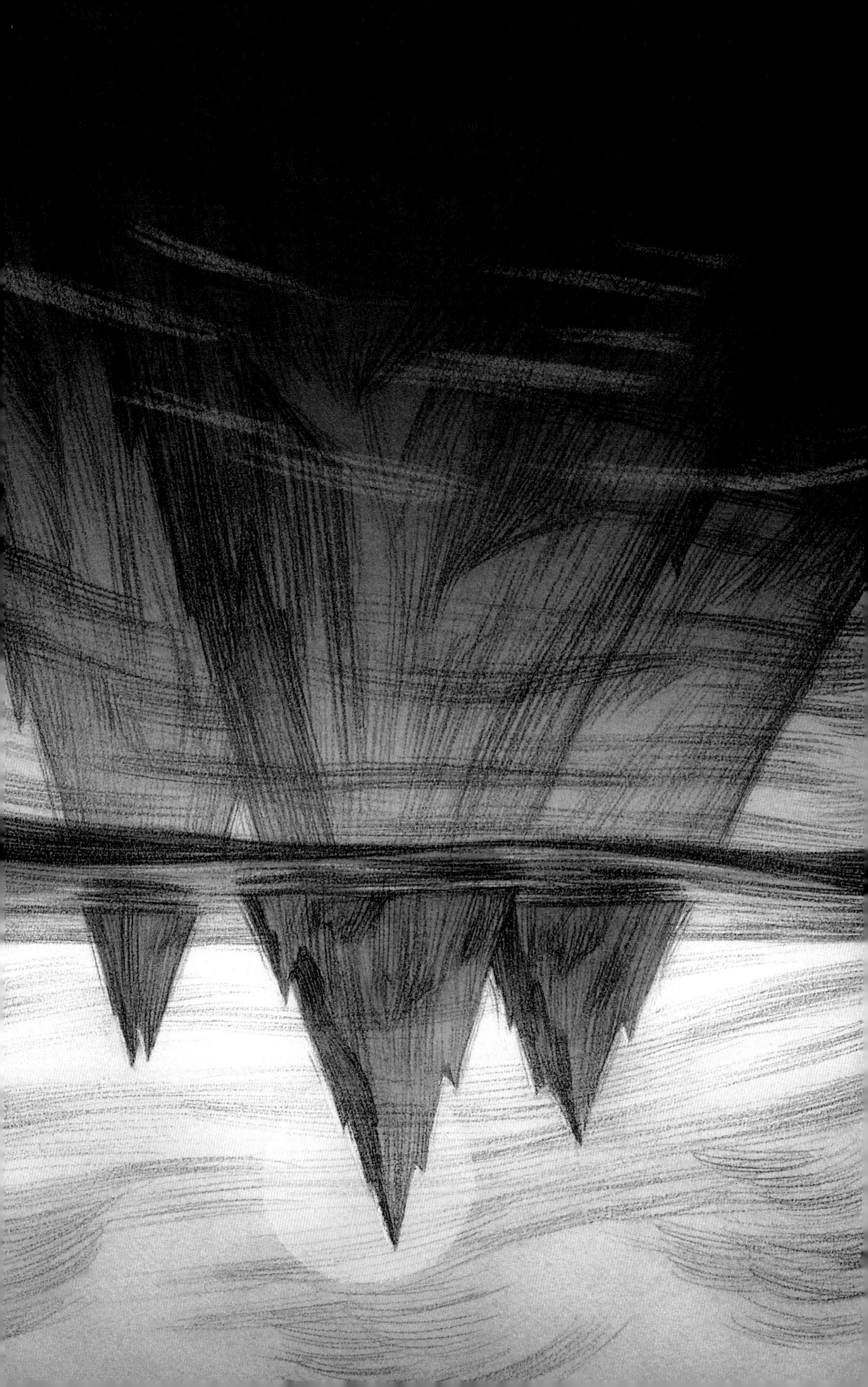

Wick will be here at the setting of the sun."

"You will live to see him defeated," the Captain said, swimming close to Demetrius. "But not a moment longer."

"You're probably right."

The Captain looked at me, surprised at Demetrius's lack of concern. "He is dolorous," I said. "Like men are known to be."

"They are weak." She swam to the stern of our ship to confer with the sailors, who were already unloading further weapons for our Captain to use: a plate for her head, blades hewn from coral for her tail. These were old, unwieldy but brutal, used only for the biggest ships and only then when coordinated in a rare tandem with another hunting pod.

There were no additional weapons for the Apprentices.

"Toby Wick will bring a fleet," Willem said, swimming next to me again. "No matter what your man says."

"Probably," I said.

"We are but one ship."

"It is a little late to be having doubts, Willem."

"I do not have doubts. I merely point out how magnificent our victory will be." She said it convincingly, as if I needed it. "Prophecy will be our greatest weapon."

"You poor foolish things," Demetrius said to me as Willem swam away on patrol. "I do not pity them." He nodded to the other whales. "But I pity you."

"You think we're doomed."

"I do not *think* it."

"His fleet will outnumber us?"

"The devil always outnumbers his foes," he said. "Even if he is alone."

"What does that mean?"

"Only rumor. Only folktale. I know as much as you. When he comes, we will see."

He was more right than he knew. For when the sun crossed the Abyss below us one last time, and night started seeping into the ocean like octopus ink, Toby Wick came.

And we did see. ◆

34

JUST AS THE SUN HIT THE HORIZON, THE famous white hull of his ship appeared around the far side of one of the islands. As simply as that.

The moment had arrived, too fast, too sudden. I felt prepared but not ready. Though perhaps that would never have been possible, had I had my whole life to know I was heading for this moment.

With a turn around a mountain, here came our devil.

"He has come alone," the Captain said, wonderingly. "Your man spoke the truth."

I looked at Demetrius, but his eyes were on Toby Wick, too, wide with terror. My own unease, already twisting my guts, grew. "I would not trust it," I said.

"You insult me if you think me a Captain who would," she said, eyes still on Toby Wick's great white hull. "Our destiny is here, my Apprentices. We have been chosen, and whether by prophecy or fate or even chance, dear Bathsheba, even you cannot deny it has arrived for us all."

"No, my Captain," I said. "I cannot."

"Lucky is the whale who meets her prophecy's end," she said. "Prepare yourselves."

These last were superfluous words. We'd had a night and a day. There was no more tactical preparation to be done. Our Captain in her armor, we two – just two – Apprentices with our harpoons, and the plan the Captain had laid out as we waited. Demetrius had no more to offer about what we might expect, but our Captain seemed to have forgotten about him altogether. The day was here. This one man could wait.

"Do you think it will hurt?" Willem said to me quietly, as we took our positions.

"What?"

"When we die. Do you think it will hurt?"

That's when I realized what was different about her, different in even the small eye that genuinely wanted an answer to this impossible question but was only interested distantly, as if in a scientific query about tides.

Her eye was the eye of a true believer.

"You believe we will die?" I asked.

"For a glorious cause. For the death of Toby Wick." Her eye glinted. "But our names. Our names shall live for evermore."

"Not if no one survives to tell the story."

A shimmer of doubt passed over her. Then our Captain's voice came like a volcano. "Our moment is here and the two of you gossip?!" She swung her tail our way, though her attention was too fixed on the approach of Toby Wick's ship to cause us any damage other than turbulence.

The ship continued its journey toward us, a decent speed along the surface of the Abyss, but nothing that could be considered fast. He was coming to us at his own rate, would enjoin the battle at a moment of his own choosing.

Or so he thought.

"Begin your ascents," the Captain ordered, and Willem and I dove for the sky. ◆

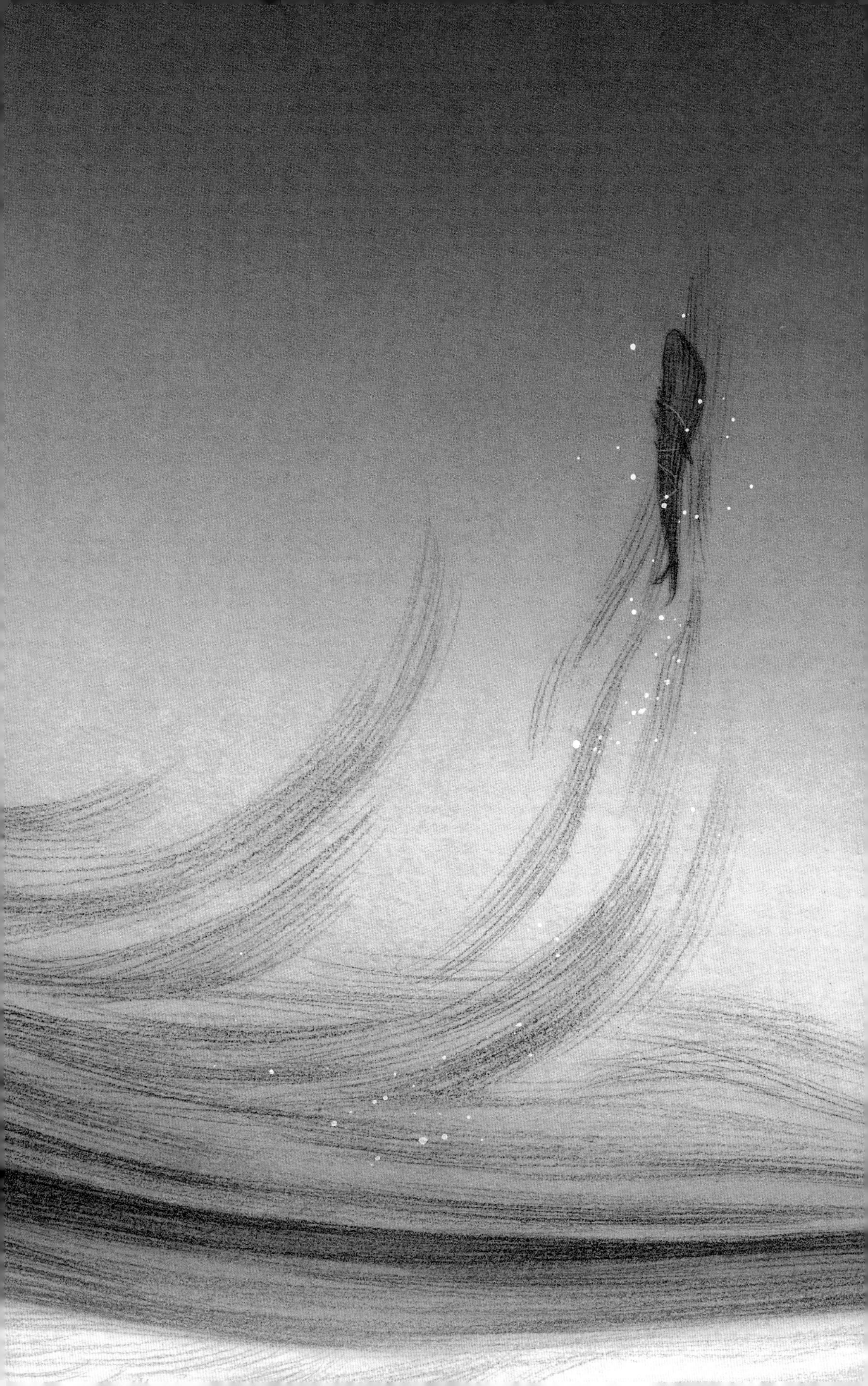

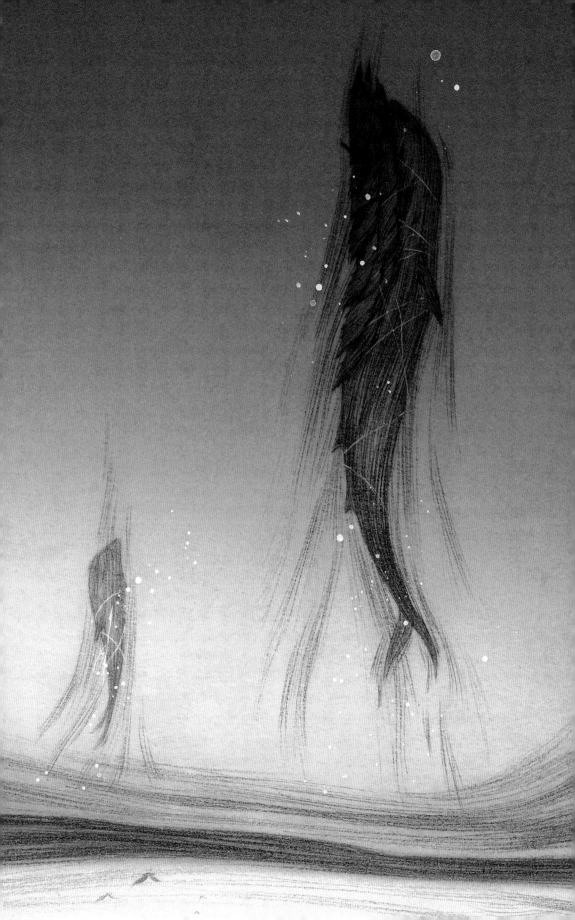

35

THE PLAN, FOR WHAT IT WAS: WILLEM
and I would ascend, deep into the sky, before turning
to make our attack run. We — two small whales in an
entire ocean to make the first strike against the mon-
strous legend of Toby Wick — we would shoot into the
Abyss on either side of Toby Wick's ship. One of us, both
of us, would certainly be killed, but his attention would
be taken for at least a moment.

Which was when our Captain would pierce the very
belly of his hull, descending like fury itself from the sky.

It was madness. It was impossible. If no other whale
had ever managed it, why would we?

Because it was prophesied?

Deep, we swam, and high. I felt the ocean's tightening
grip. I strained my eyes for city lights in the miles around,
even sent echolocation to try and feel the shapes of the
homes and work-spaces of my people. The lights we'd cre-
ated from luminescent life-forms. The oxygen wells, larger
versions of our breather bubbles, really, but an innovation
that had nearly — nearly — liberated us from the surface of
the Abyss altogether. I called out for my people, sending
no message except the forever message: *I am here, are you here?*

But there was no answer. Aside from the islands, this part of the sky was empty.

We were alone.

"Turn," we heard. Our Captain, diving between us, past us, deeper and deeper. Her own turn would come later. Her power all that much greater.

Willem and I swung back toward the surface of the Abyss in fast curves. We raced downward now, feeling the pressure loosen, feeling the air in our lungs and breather bubbles expand as we approached the treacherous air of men.

"Aim for starboard," Willem said.

"I know," I said.

"I'll surface from the port side."

"I *know*."

"May this day be glorious. May this be the day our names are remembered."

"I already remember your name, Willem. Wilhelmina."

"It was foretold."

"Only once it already happened."

We dove and dove, down and down and down, our tails making the currents boil. The Abyss drew closer, closer still. I saw our own ship, the *Alexandra*, my home for nearly a year, off to my left, the sailors watching the attack as we made it, echolocations of encouragement chirping their way through the water.

I saw Demetrius there, still tied to the mast. I wondered if I would keep my promise to him. I wondered what promise I had actually made.

The Abyss grew pink as the sun started to leave it, the water near the surface still holding the last lights of day.

And it was in that light that we saw.

"*No,*" I heard Willem say, in horror.

"Call off the attack!" I said, veering hard from my path.

"No!" Willem again, though in answer to me or still in her own dawning terror, I did not know, nor did she live for me to find out.

Because we both saw it as we neared, too late to stop, too late in realizing our mistake.

The great white hull wasn't Toby Wick's ship.

It was Toby Wick himself. ◆

36

ONE GIANT FIST REACHED FROM THE ABYSS, from where we now saw he had been hiding them, and grabbed Willem round the middle. I heard only the briefest yelp before she was ripped from the water. A few seconds later her blood poured into the ocean and her body landed with a splash, broken, nearly torn in two.

I barely had time to register it, as Toby Wick's other arm was already reaching for me, our plan to attack from either side clearly the worst possible. I dodged a great thumb and fingers, but he caught my tail briefly, pulling off half my fin as if it were so much seaweed. I tumbled toward our ship, screaming from the pain.

I managed to get near Demetrius. "How did you not tell us this?" I shouted at him in the maelstrom.

He looked at me, utterly shocked. "I did not *know*. There were stories but–"

"He is the devil."

"Bathsheba," he said.

It was his last word, as the great white body of Toby Wick blocked out the last of the sun. I struggled away from the ship as the devil made short work of our sailors, killing them as easily as if they were the shoals of squid from which we made our meals.

And then.

And then.

His terrible, terrible face. Dipping up into the ocean

itself, grimacing barnacle-encrusted teeth as big as my head, wild eyes open in the salt, looking round, blazing with a madness that brooked no mercy, no argument, a mouth smiling in triumph as he grasped for the ship. His hair trailed behind him as he reached, great kelp beds from which coral grew and sharks swam.

That's when I saw it.

He was whale. Arms, yes, the face and features of a man, but also somehow whale. A whale of the Abyss. A whale who was our reflection in monstrousness. And also a man who was a reflection of men's, too. A place like the surface of the water where our worlds met.

It's no wonder he slaughtered us. It's no wonder he slaughtered *them*.

As now, when he crushed the ship like a toy.

"Demetrius!" I heard myself call, struggling to keep my orientation with the injury to my tail. I tell myself, even now, all these years later, that I would have swam toward him had I not been so injured, but I still also wonder if that's true. Would I have been able to overcome my terror to try and save this one man? To try and almost certainly fail?

He looked over at me as the great fists of Toby Wick came for him. He did not speak. His last word had been my name. The last word he heard was me speaking his own.

Did this mean anything? And if it only meant something for the two of us, did that reduce it? For I felt the same give inside me that I felt when I found the body of the child. I felt a rip as he went to his death.

"Demetrius," I said again, but softly, quietly, only to myself, as Toby Wick took him in his hands. I saw Demetrius's face as he died. It was filled with relief.

And a kind of worship.

Then I was alone in the ocean with the devil.

Here was prophecy. Here was prophecy incarnate. And now I saw the truth. Every attack we attributed to him – from the massacre of my mother to, yes, the men who had harpooned and released my Captain – only brought the legend to life. You imagine the devil, you *make* the devil.

He broke our mast, ripped up the deck, sent the contents of our hull plummeting up to the darkest deep. Only the body of Demetrius floated to the Abyss, where all bodies that breathe air, ours included, go.

Toby Wick turned for me.

And our Captain flew out of the darkness, piercing him through the stomach. ◆

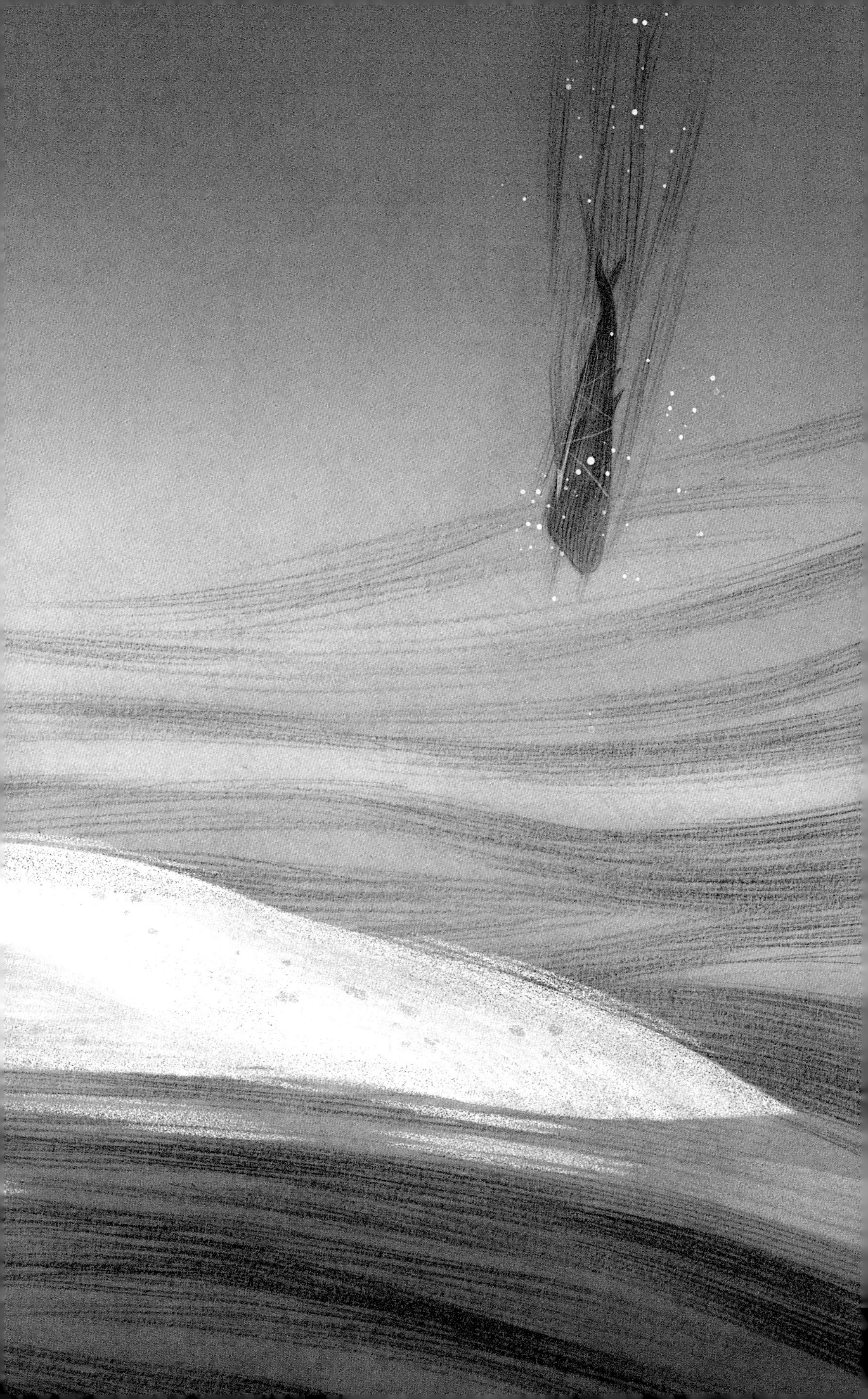

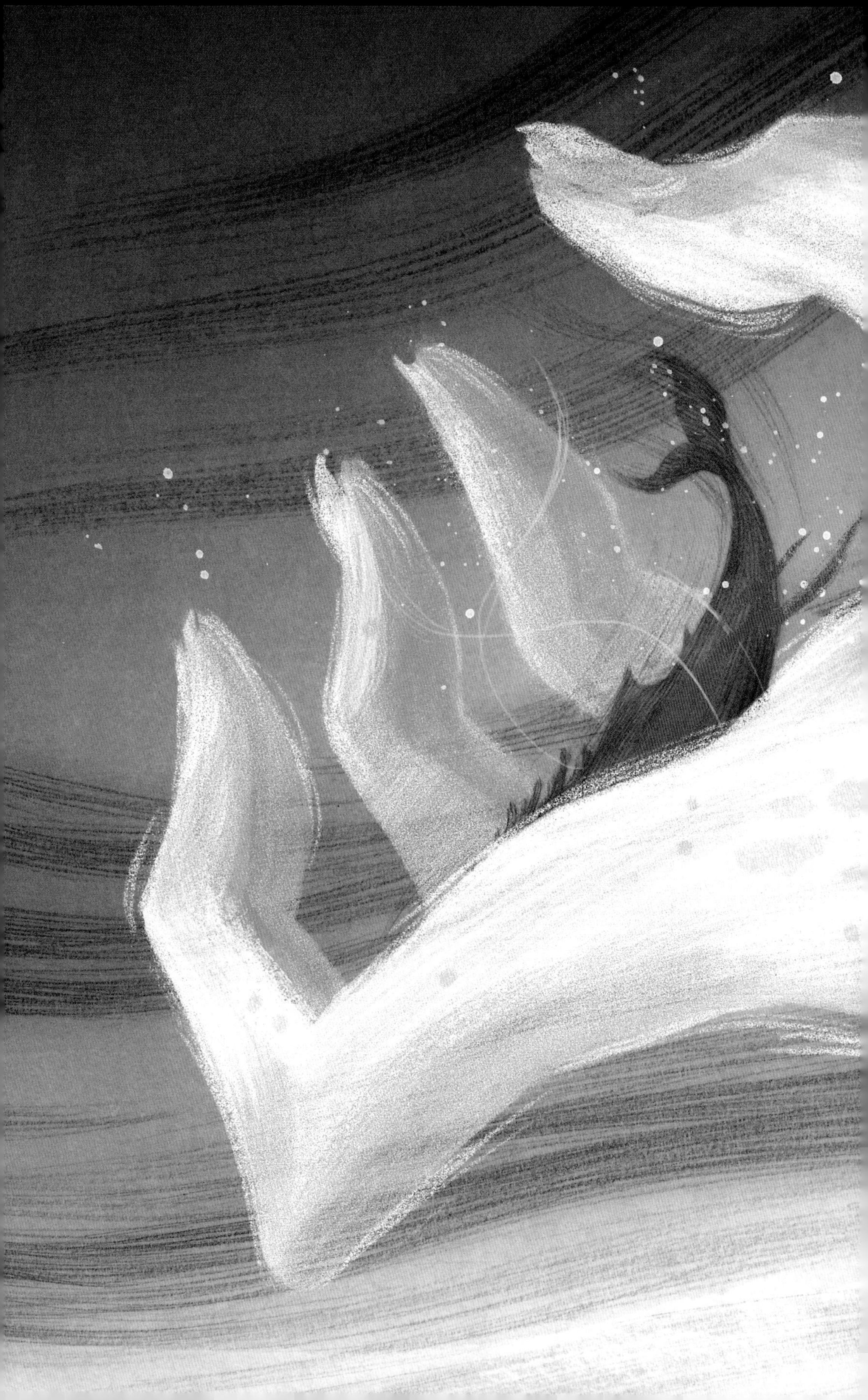

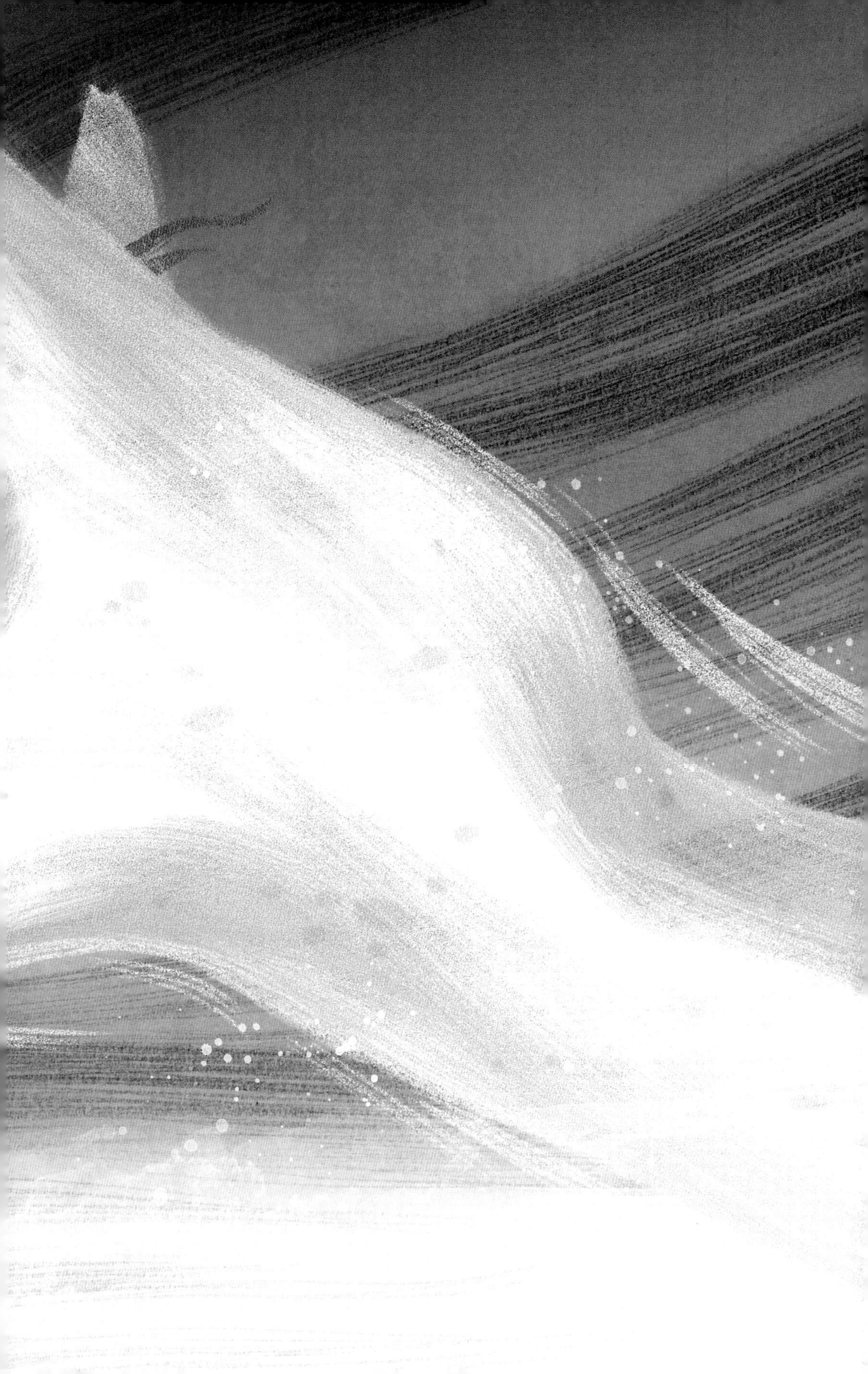

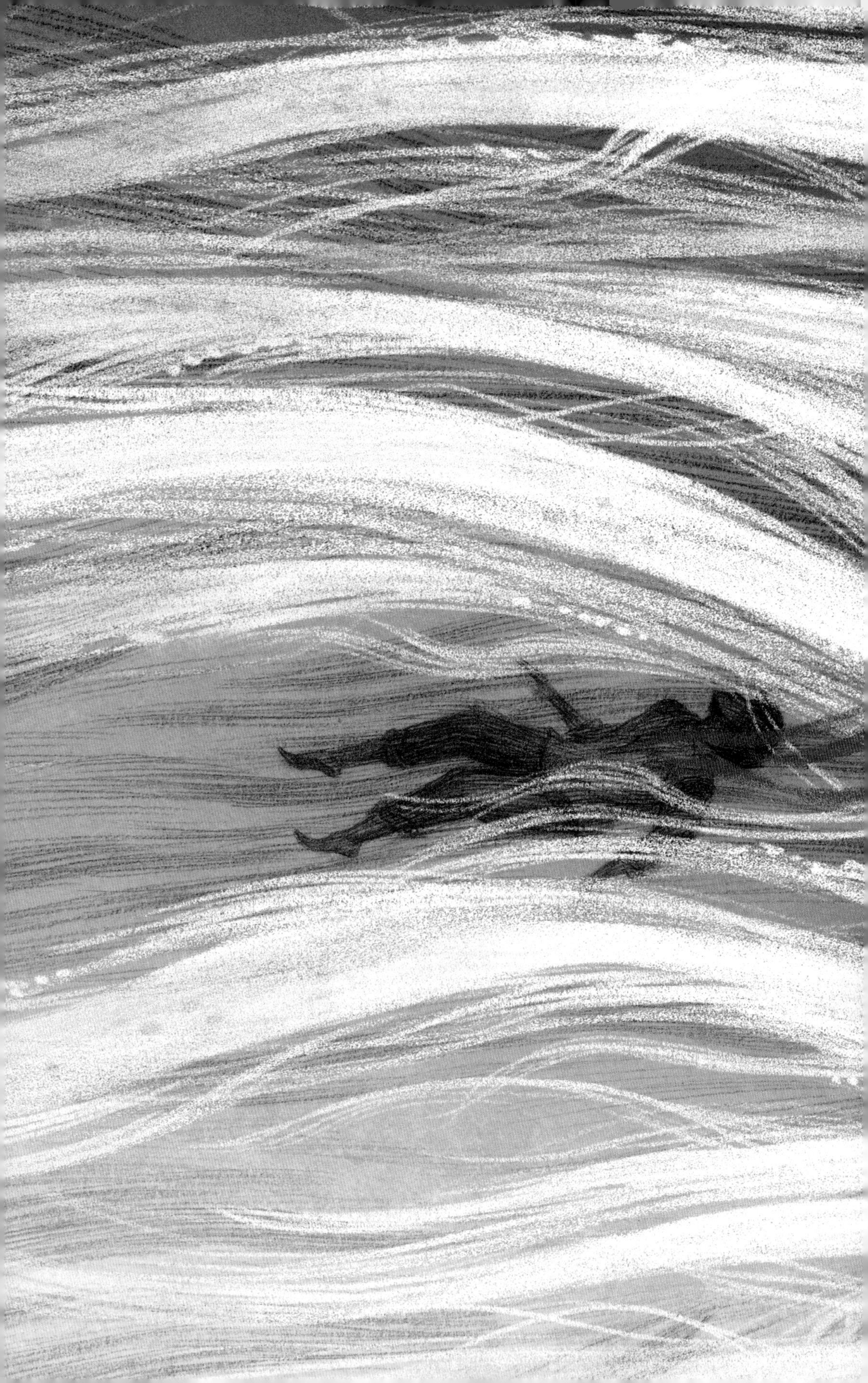

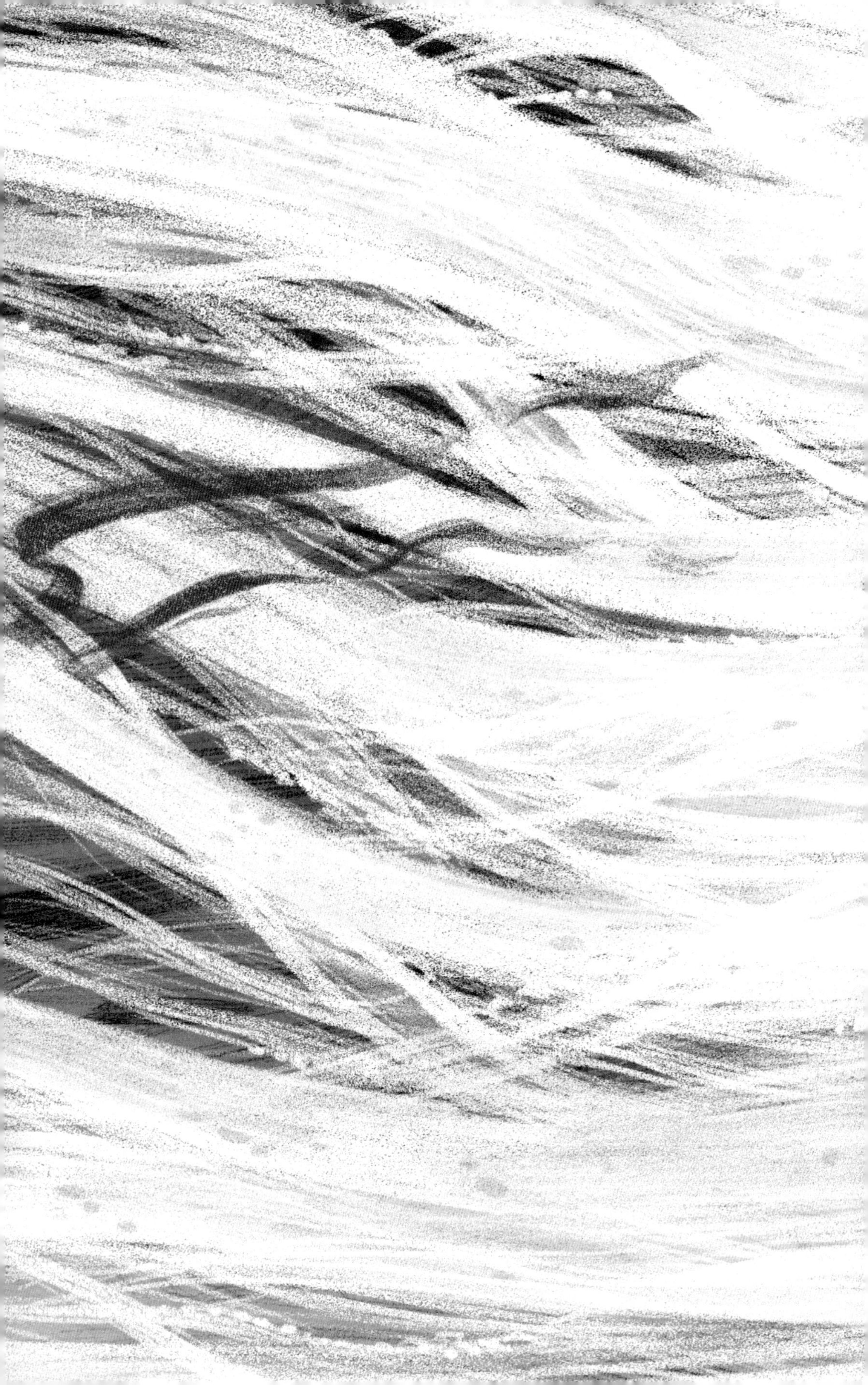

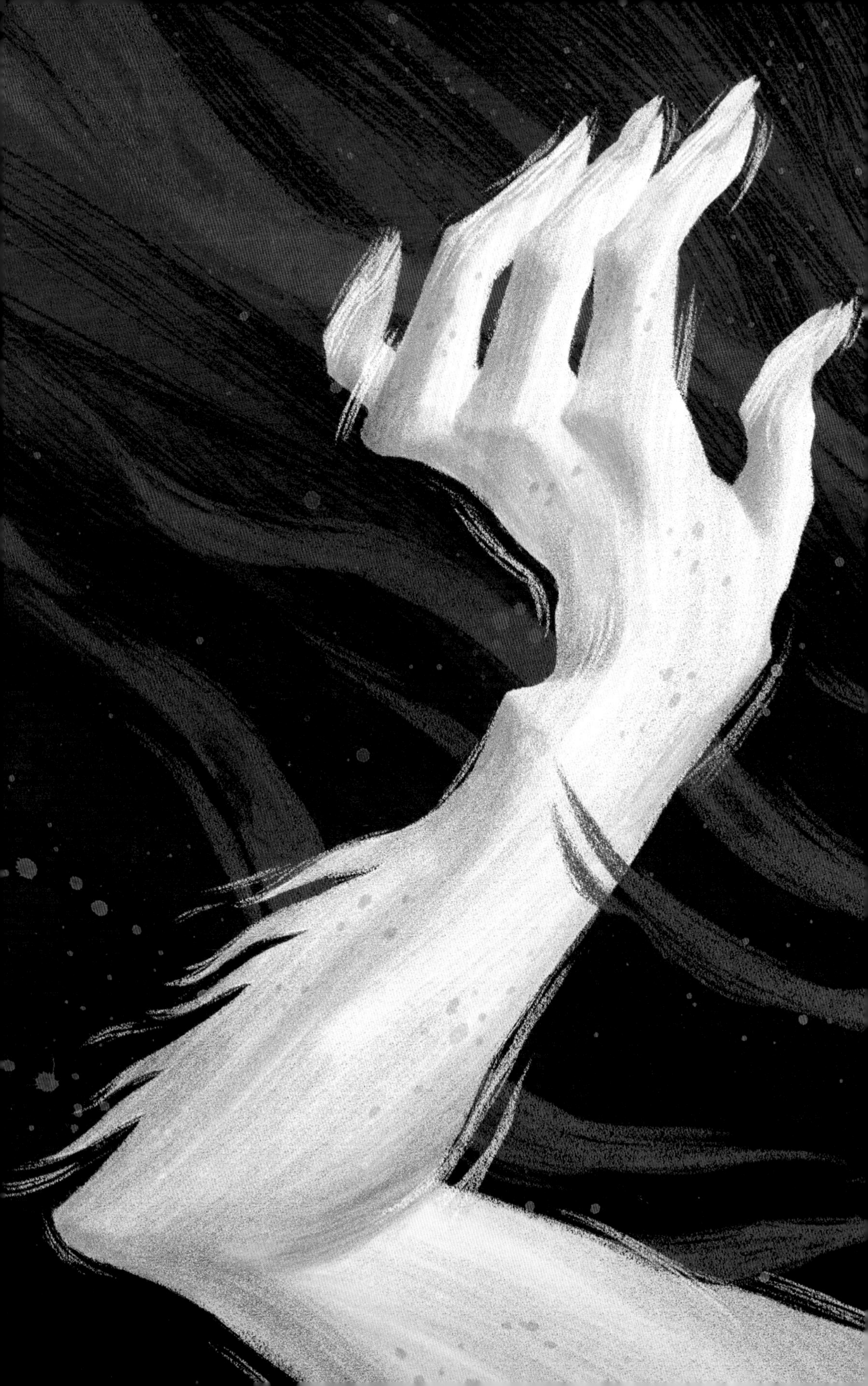

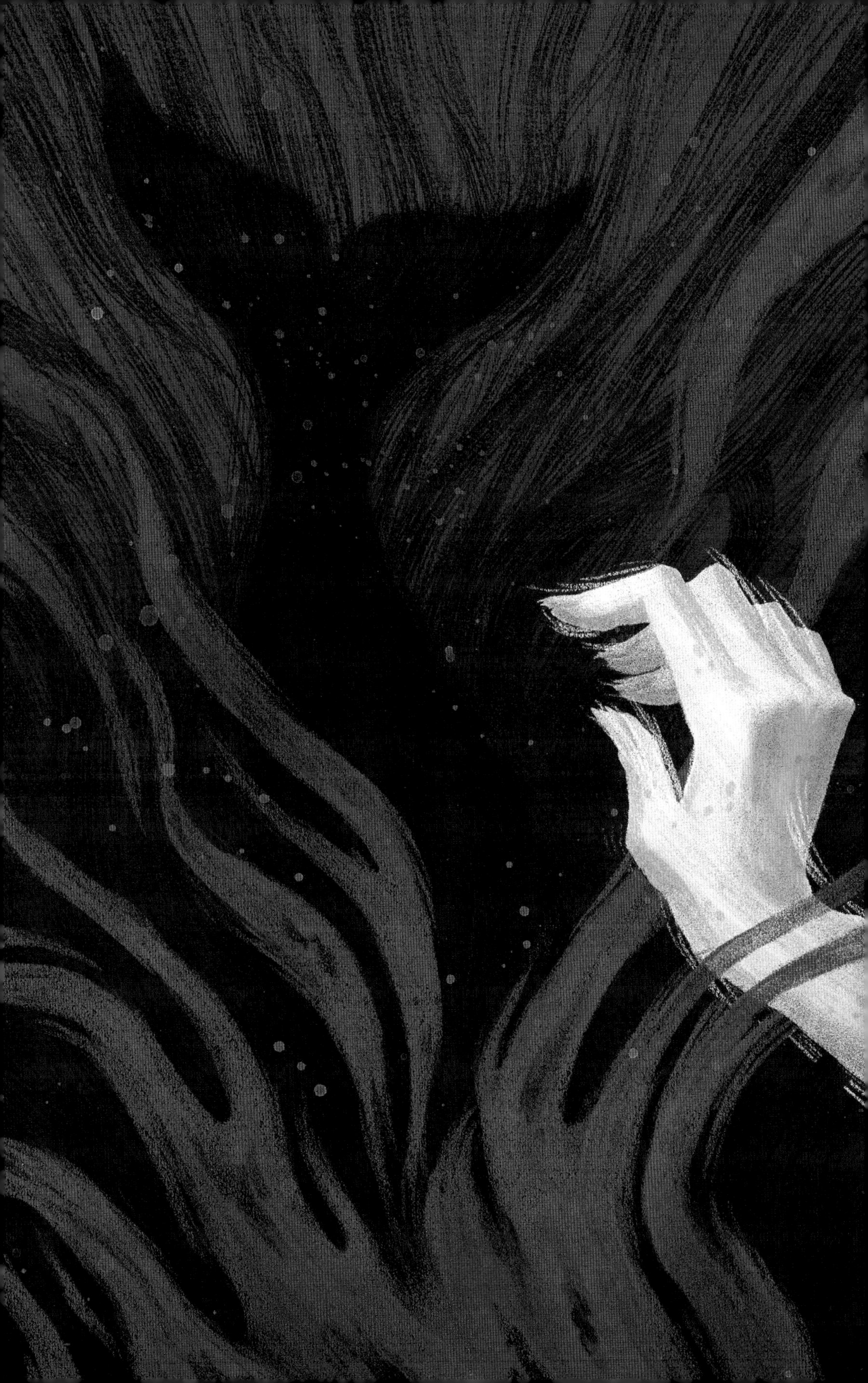

37

THOUGH HIS ROAR WAS MADE OF AIR, bubbles raging from his open mouth, it was loud enough to temporarily deafen me.

Nothing stopped my eyes, though.

Impossibly, even in this chaos, even with this unimaginable price, the Captain's plan was working. Willem was dead, the sailors were dead, Demetrius, too, but as Toby Wick was momentarily distracted with putting me among their number, Captain Alexandra of the lost ship *Alexandra* hit him hard enough, fast enough, to buck him into the Abyss.

Blood flooded around her, so thick I could only see her tail churning against it, pushing herself further into him. I can only imagine that, upon seeing what he was, upon glimpsing the horror that had lured us here with clever tricks and clues, she knew she had just the one chance, the one landing of the weapon of herself.

For his hands were already reaching for her, his huge body twisting in the water to force her up toward the Abyss. He grabbed her small dorsal fin in one great hand, but then let go with another roar as the Captain must have struck something deep inside him, churning his guts with that shield on her nose, perhaps even with the rusty harpoon that men had left inside her.

He grabbed at her again, her tail in both his fists, the two of them spinning in the water as she continued to push and he continued to kick with legs longer than my former ship. They were becoming one in the water, the Captain disappearing inside him. He called out again as she hurt him, as his hands sought her.

And then he looked to me again.

Eyes larger than those of the giant squid we fought in the depths, a grotesque and broken nose, and those teeth that gnashed and bit at the water as if to chew it to pieces.

The devil himself favored me with his gaze.

What can I say about this? How can I explain it? The horror of him, but the *power* of him . . .

And oh oh oh, to my shame, to my bafflement, to my *anguish*, I was drawn. My will slipped away from me as I looked into those eyes, as one hand reached out again to me, not to catch me this time, just the forefingers beckoning me near.

To do what? Help him kill the Captain? Be killed myself? I did not know then and I do not know now. I only know that, with half my tail fin missing, with the very ocean turning to blood, with the bodies of my crewmates around me, I began to falteringly swim toward Toby Wick, answering his call, as if all my choices had been made for me and this was the final one—

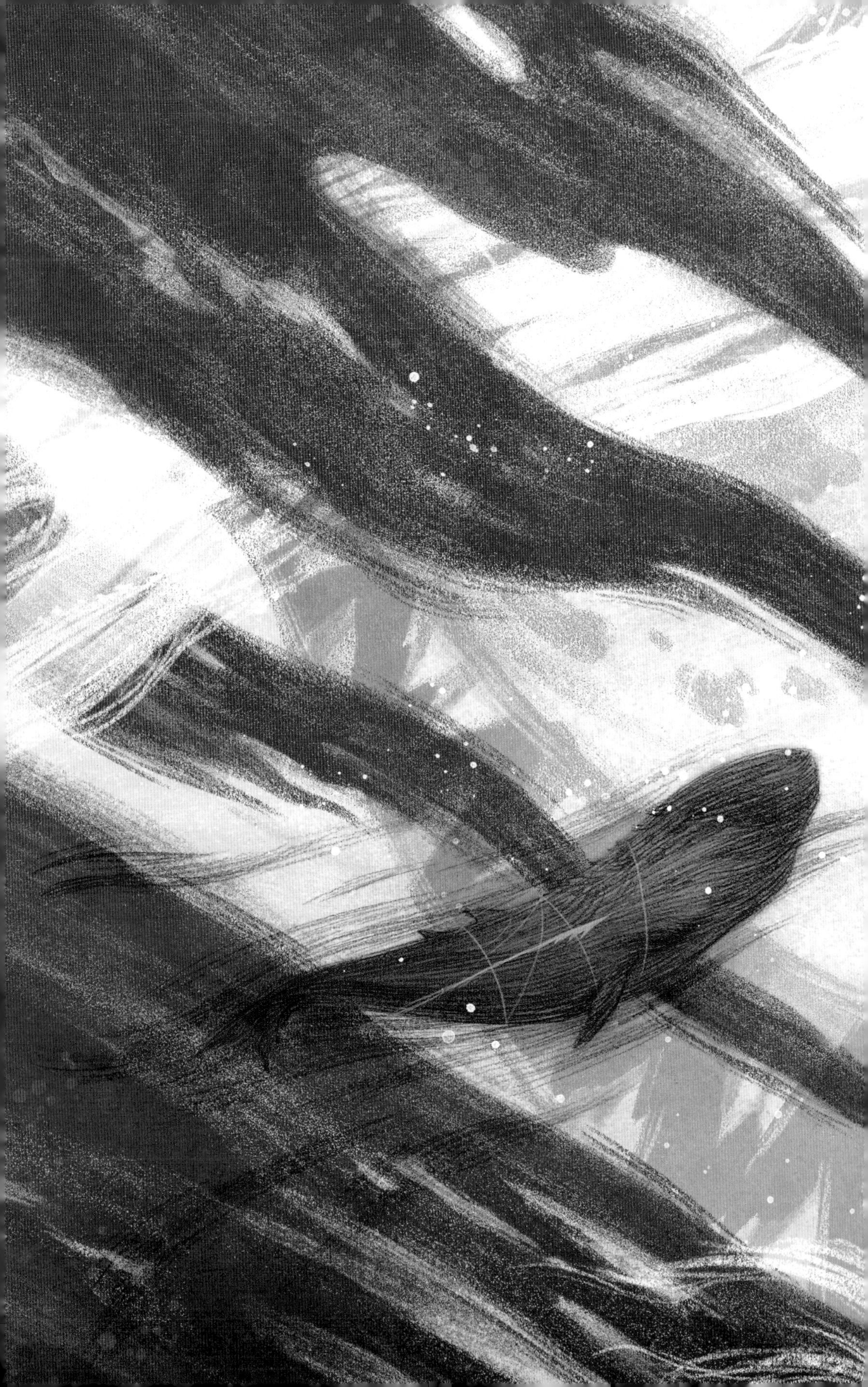

But then he convulsed at another tear from our Captain. His hands went back to her, but he could not get her free, struggle though he might.

The blood was now coming from his mouth as well. He still fought as she tenaciously refused to let him go, digging deeper and deeper into him, causing him to roll.

And here is where I lost them. They disappeared into a cloud of thickening blood, growing farther and farther from me, staining the sea as they went. I tried to follow, but the wound in my own tail made me slow. I still tried, only stopping when out of the fury of blood emerged my Captain's entire pectoral fin.

That was the last I saw of her.

That was the last anyone saw of Toby Wick.

So fast I could barely comprehend it, I was alone in an empty ocean, with my tail injured and no prophecy to be found anywhere at all. ◆

38

IT WAS, AS YOU KNOW, AS YOU *ALL* KNOW, Captain Arcturus who found me, scenting blood in the water, fighting off the sharks that grew bold at my weakness. And though his words are regularly scorned because he spoke "mercy" to my Captain, it is also true that the war with men has been over since that day. A new peace dawned. Our pods were no longer slaughtered. Men's ships no longer wrecked.

For all these long decades, peace has reigned. No formal treaty, no declarations. Just that most powerful cultural control of all: rumor. Even when no one would take Captain Arcturus seriously, rumors still spread, rumors of what had happened. I had told him the story but also that he must keep my name unknown, that I would not admit to being a part of it until the day it was necessary.

That day has come.

The bodies of Toby Wick and our Captain were never found. As the time has passed, as our strength has grown, as we have avoided men on the surface of the Abyss, as they have avoided *us*, the vividity of old rumors died away.

Now, new rumors have begun.

A rumor of the return of Toby Wick.

And perhaps that's all it will take to bring him back.

This is why I never spoke before. A disgraced Captain like Arcturus would never be afforded something as powerful as a prophecy to his name. But a Third Apprentice, who became a Second Apprentice, who – I suppose – with the death of Willem and Captain Alexandra, became First Apprentice and even Captain of a destroyed ship? A whale who spoke with a man long enough to discover he was a baker, a whale who lost her mother and part of her tail, then watched everyone she knew die at the hands of the devil?

A whale who had nearly answered the devil's own beckoning?

Oh, her name would carry prophecy down the ages. Her name would be the foundation for an inevitable future. Signs would be read. Hindsight would confirm those signs.

Who knows what new devils we might create?

And so now I tell you my story. Now is the time. For rumors swirl and oceans stir and in that maelstrom, I fear, devils will rise. Are rising. Have risen. The great trick of the devil is to make you want to see him. But it is only when you *see* him that you fear him. And by then, it is too late.

As, I fear, *I* might be. We are too eager to build devils. Is it only a matter of time before we are at war again?

So I beg of you. Take the name Bathsheba. Take it and place on it the prophecy of *not* going down this road. Take my name as the warning of where our fears will lead us, where the devils we make will destroy us all. Or take

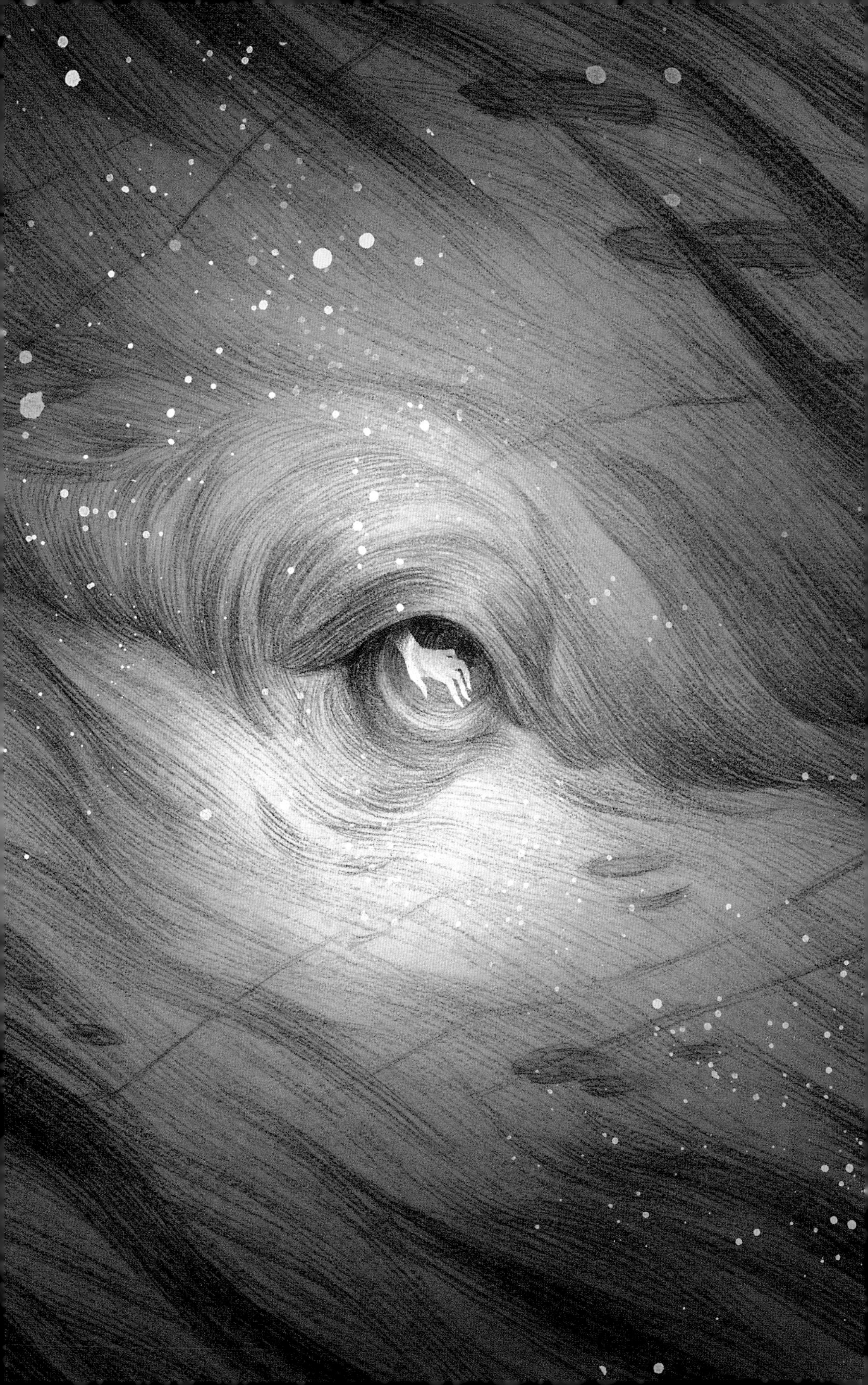

it as what might happen if a whale can learn the name of a man, and he can learn hers. And she can mourn at his passing. If this is possible, what else might be?

Take these prophecies, I beg you, take them in the shape of my broken heart. We have had these years of peace, why should we choose to abandon them? Why should you swim so quickly to break your heart alongside mine?

And yet here is news of a pod being massacred out in the deep ocean. A pod no one has seen but all have heard of.

Here is news of a new story beginning.

Let my name be the prophecy of how that story ends. Not in glory, but in death.

Take this name. Take Bathsheba and make it a story of peace.

For there are devils in the deep,
but worst are the ones
we make.

◆